AND WHERE
BEEN ALL

"Albert." Unlike certain previo̲u̲s̲ ̲w̲i̲v̲e̲s̲—Al wondered suddenly how many previous wives he'd had in this particular timeline—her use of his name indicated great patience and a certain amount of humor.

He closed his eyes and shook his head. "It's nothing, really."

It occurred to him, all of a sudden, that he could probably resolve this mess simply by taking the handlink and going back into the Imaging Chamber and encouraging Sam to do something. Anything. Lord only knew what small things would change the future. A dead butterfly in the Cretaceous could lead to a new world government; doubtless Sam Beckett's choice of breakfast beverage could get Al Calavicci out of an unexpected marriage. . . .

Janna smiled at him.

Well. He didn't have to change things right away, did he? It could always wait until morning. Couldn't it? . . .

QUANTUM LEAP

OUT OF TIME. OUT OF BODY.
OUT OF CONTROL.

QUANTUM LEAP

RANDOM MEASURES

A NOVEL BY

ASHLEY McCONNELL

**BASED ON THE UNIVERSAL TELEVISION
SERIES *QUANTUM LEAP*
CREATED BY DONALD P. BELLISARIO**

ACE BOOKS, NEW YORK

Quantum Leap: Random Measures,
a novel by Ashley McConnell, based on the
Universal television series QUANTUM LEAP,
created by Donald P. Bellisario.

This book is an Ace original edition,
and has never been previously published.

QUANTUM LEAP: RANDOM MEASURES

An Ace Book / published by arrangement with
MCA Publishing Rights, a Division of MCA, Inc.

PRINTING HISTORY
Ace edition / March 1995

ISBN: 0-441-00182-3

ACE®
Ace Books are published by The Berkley Publishing Group,
200 Madison Avenue, New York, NY 10016.
ACE and the "A" design are trademarks
belonging to Charter Communications, Inc.

PRINTED IN THE UNITED STATES OF AMERICA

10 9 8 7 6 5 4 3 2 1

To the memory of Dennis
Wolfberg, a fine actor who will be sincerely
missed by all the fans of *Quantum Leap*

ACKNOWLEDGMENTS

Thanks for this one go to the ever-merciful and understanding editors, Ginjer Buchanan and Nancy Cushing-Jones, and to Kathy Mclaren, Anne Wasserman, Kim Round, Lisa Winters (woof woof) and Arianwen, Nancy Holder, John Donne, all those who hang out in Those Topics on GEnie, and all the people I meant to acknowledge all along.

A foolish consistency is the hobgoblin of little minds, adored by little statesmen and philosophers and divines.

—Ralph Waldo Emerson

PROLOGUE

Somewhere in time . . .

No man is an island, entire of itself; every man is
a piece of the continent, a part of the main; . . .
any man's death diminishes mc, because I am
involved in mankind . . .
  —John Donne, Devotions XVII

Wind in his face. Sunlight.

He wobbled, clenched a rope under his hand and caught
himself. Nylon fibers bit into his palm. Ignoring them, he
looked around and laughed, delighted. He was standing in
the air.

Well, almost—Al was standing in the air; Sam Beckett
was balanced precariously on the rounded wicker edge of a
hot air balloon gondola, shivering in a cold thin breeze, as
close to floating as he had ever been. He could remember
being afraid of heights as if the fear mattered to someone
else, but up here, up in the perfect silence of the upper
sky, the ground had nothing to do with him. He could look
down and see carefully groomed fields, Impressionist trees,
mitelike cars crawling along lines of highway, and none of
it had to do with Sam Beckett. He was the center of a
painting, a panorama. Below him was the earth; around
him, the sky.

1

A raven floated by, teetering on the wind, and looked him over with bright black eyes. He reached out with his free hand. The bird squawked indignantly and tilted away to glide on a convenient thermal at a safer distance.

"Er, Sam, don't do that," Al advised him. The Observer was concentrating on the handlink, punching a series of patterns on the colored cubes, frowning with pursed lips, trying another series. The wind failed to ruffle his hair, to flutter his rich dark forest green suit with the matching dark green-and-gold brocade vest.

Sam glanced at the man standing on nothing and laughed again. "It's like flying!" he cried. He didn't even bother to look to check who he was or what he was wearing this time; he was having too much fun simply looking around at the world.

Behind him, someone else in the gondola laughed in agreement. Sam twisted around to see who shared his delight. A woman in her late twenties, clinging to the opposite side of the wickerwork basket that held them both, smiled widely at him. Sam grinned back.

"Yeah," Al grunted, not looking up. "Hmmm. Sam, clip that thing there."

"What thing?" If Al was in a Mood, Sam was willing to humor him. He made a mental note to go hot-air ballooning again, and hoped that he'd remember.

"What?" the woman echoed. Sam could see his own exhilaration reflected in her eyes as she reached for a lever. "Are you ready?" she said.

"That thing there." Still not looking up, Al pointed with his ever-present cigar to a large metal clip hanging over the edge of the basket.

"Okay, fine." Sam grabbed the clip, snapped it onto a strap hanging over the nearest piece of gondola, and looked up just as the blower roared to life. The sound was earsplitting; heat slapped at his face and hands. Tongues of fire, nearly colorless against the sky, shot straight up into the mouth of the balloon. Leaning his head back and squinting against

2

the temperature-distortion of the atmosphere, he could see rippling silk panels in jewel tones of red and green meeting in a small open circle, high overhead.

But it was nothing, nothing to the expanse of horizon all around him. The blower shut down, and the balloon floated silent again, serene among the white mountains of the air. He reached out, only half believing the cold wetness in his palm. "I touched it," he exulted. "I touched the clouds!"

"Ahuh," Al said, still busily jabbing. He spared a glance to the cloud, which was drifting through his left shoe, and shook his foot automatically to free it. The raven circled him, squawked once, and flapped away. "Nyyyaaahhhh," the hologram jeered after it.

He could see the curvature of the earth, Sam thought, if he tried. He could calculate how high he had to be to really see it, but he didn't want to waste the moment with mere calculation. He wanted to step off the wickerwork and spread his arms and follow the raven.

As if in answer to his wish, the woman behind him said, "You're sure you're ready?"

He answered, "Yes!"

And a solid shove in the small of his back sent him off the edge of the gondola and spiraling down—down, down to the manicured fields, the tiny matchbox cars rapidly becoming larger, and the glory of standing in the sky was abruptly replaced by sheer helpless terror. He slapped at himself desperately, looking for a parachute that wasn't there, and tried unsuccessfully to kick. He couldn't. The earth spun beneath him, the tiny images growing, expanding, as if the planet were stretching its maw wide to swallow him.

As he screamed Al descended beside him, ruffled not one whit by the fall, still concentrating on the handlink. Sam retained enough presence of mind to duck his chin in toward his chest, getting his mouth out of the windstream, and yell, "Al! Do something!"

Al looked up, took the cigar out of his mouth, and asked reasonably, "What?"

3

Sam looked down at the whirling earth and screamed again. The wind of his fall dragged at his face, his clothing, whistled in his ears. Hair whipped into his eyes as the earth rushed up to meet him. It wasn't fair, he thought, it wasn't right, he *couldn't* die this way, not now, not with his Observer right there and apparently unperturbed; he'd gone too far, done too many things, he wanted to go *home,* and he hit the end of the bungee cord with a terrific jolt and jerked back upward with Al still beside him, not a lock of hair out of place, and hit the top of the arc to see the balloon with the pilot waving enthusiastically, and fell again, and hit the end of the cord and swung upward, with Al, still beside him all the way, griping, "I wish to heck you'd Leap, Sam. I haven't been this dizzy since I took zero-gravity in astronaut training," and above them the woman in the balloon looked over the edge of the gondola, cheering, and all Sam could say as he ricocheted through the clouds was "Oh boy . . . *OY* . . . oy . . . *OY* . . . oy . . ."

And mercifully, Leaped.

FRIDAY

June 6, 1975

Thou art slave to fate, chance. . . .
—John Donne, Holy Sonnets IX

CHAPTER ONE

He was still dizzy, and carrying a weight on one shoulder, and it was dark, and the footing was wet and slippery, as if it had recently rained. It wasn't surprising that he stumbled.

This time, he couldn't even remember being in that other place, waiting for an identity, a Voice. This time he had fallen directly into his next Leap. Fallen . . . He caught his breath and a nearby tree trunk and shook for a few minutes, fighting residual panic, grateful for the weight he carried if only because it pressed him firmly against the solid ground.

Maybe whoever was in charge of his ricocheting through Time—God or Fate or Chance, Time or Whatever—thought that bungee jumping from a hot air balloon was just one of those interesting things he should be made to do occasionally for his own good. The fact that he was still shuddering inside from the terror of free fall was irrelevant. He glared up at the sky. "Thanks a *lot*."

"Hey, you haven't earned your tip yet," a slurry voice said from ahead of him and slightly to his right. "Let's get that l'il keg over here before you drop it, okay?"

Sam took two more steps forward and found himself in a wide clearing lit by a pair of roaring campfires. Some thirty young people were sitting or standing around, perhaps half of them looking at him expectantly. He could smell cooking

7

meat and burning vegetation and water and pine trees.

By this time he was used to doing a rapid, almost unconscious assessment of Who Am I Where Am I What Am I. He gathered data without even being aware of the process: jeans/heavy laced boots/flannel shirt/"keg" = probably male, probably young; details like personal appearance he could check out later on. Luckily it wasn't a full-sized keg. Quarter, he estimated. A baby keg. But damned heavy, nonetheless.

The others gathered by the fires, standing or sitting on deck chairs or blankets to protect themselves from the muddy ground, were all about the same age, in their late teens. They all wore slacks cut suspiciously full from the knee down, and variations on T-shirts and long crocheted vests. He automatically noted the fashions, wishing he were a computer using parallel processing so he could check them against a mental database while simultaneously keeping on his feet. At least the vertigo from the balloon jump was fading.

There was a definite nip in the air. Sam could feel himself drawn to the warmth of the fire, bright flames against the darkness, smaller cousin of the flames that provided enough hot air to keep a balloon sailing proudly through the clouds.

"Hey, bo, put it over there," a young male voice instructed him. Still disoriented from the bungee jump, Sam carried the keg over to a rack set up between the two campfires and set it down, rubbing his shoulder. He didn't care what condition this body was in, putting the cask down was a relief. It must hold seven or eight gallons of beer. He wondered whether these kids were planning to drink it all.

The owner of the voice, a boy/man sporting bushy light brown sideburns and a sneer, was waiting when he turned around, fingering bills out of a wallet. "Four bucks, right, with the delivery?" he said.

"Yeah, that sounds about right." Sam had no clue whether it was right or not. From the look in the

8

kid's eye and the snigger he cast over his shoulder, Sam was being shortchanged. Well, it wasn't his fault he didn't know the going price in these parts. He hadn't figured out where these parts were yet. Or when, for that matter.

He was up in the mountains, though, he could tell that much. The air was thinner, and the pine looked right. Not western mountains; somewhere back east, he thought, judging from the undergrowth he'd slogged through to get to the party. He'd have to find a newspaper, or a phone book, or a map. Preferably a newspaper, so he could pin down the date, too.

Meanwhile he took the proffered money and wondered what he was supposed to do next. Go back the way he came, presumably. He started off in that direction, hoping desperately for a clue to his location, his identity, what he was supposed to be doing, anything.

One of the kids staggered as he passed, almost fell into the nearer fire, and he reached out and grabbed without thinking, pulling the boy to safety. Nobody else reacted, except to laugh. He set the kid back on his feet and looked at him more closely, and then around at the others.

They were all drunk, every one of them. Not a little drunk, either. The ones on their feet were barely standing up. The boy he'd pulled out of the fire was swaying, giggling, and Sam caught him again just in time to lower him to the ground before he fell there.

Over at the edge of the clearing, one of the girls turned suddenly and vomited into a bush.

"Oh, boy," Sam said in utter disgust. And then he looked at the keg again, and realized his own part in the party. Or at least, his host's part. "Oh, *boy.*"

He was dizzy, off balance; suddenly he wasn't carrying the keg any more, and it wasn't dark. The air didn't even smell right. A split second later he realized he was flat on his back looking up at a plain white plastic-looking ceiling, and the breeze on his face was artificial, from air conditioning.

He sat up slowly and looked around.

He was in a bed, and all kinds of monitors were stuck to him, with wires leading to a bank of instruments behind him. Over against one wall, some twenty feet away, a set of stairs led up to an observation deck, glassed in. Lights on the machines up there were going crazy, blinking on and off. He wasn't wearing anything under the covers, as far as he could tell.

He shook his head and squeezed his eyes shut, cautiously opening them again after a count of ten. Nothing had changed.

It must be a hospital of some kind, but how had he gotten here? He didn't feel sick or hurt, except maybe a sore spot on his arm where an IV tube was taped in place. And the only times he'd ever been to a hospital it was just to the emergency room, and there were doctors running around all over the place, and the place stank of blood and fear and medicine, and there was always lots of shouting and confusion, people sitting in chairs by the walls crying, arguing with nurses at the desk about insurance. It wasn't like this.

This was quiet, as if somebody'd wrapped cotton wool around his ears, and empty. He was alone except for the machinery with the blinking lights.

Throwing the sheets aside, he swung his legs over the edge of the bed and peeled the sensors off his chest and legs. He was getting the last of them when he happened to look down and really see his torso.

He didn't remember having that much hair on his chest.

And he knew for certain he wasn't that pale.

There were a few other things that weren't quite the way he remembered them, either. He opened his mouth to ask the empty room what the heck was going on when a door just outside his peripheral vision opened, and he looked up to see a tall black woman dressed in a deep red dashiki sweep in. His first instinct was to demand, "Who are *you*?"

He heard the woman say, "Ziggy! Class three, stat!"

10

And then something warm hit him in the face and he folded over, not even having time to cover himself back up again, and the white room faded away.

The woman in the red dashiki paused several feet away until another woman's voice, from out of nowhere, advised, "The atmosphere is clear, Doctor." The air pressure creating a minor wind at her back—a wind that had kept the gas from her in the first place—abated. She strode over to the recumbent form, sprawled on the floor beside the examination bed, and sighed. "Well. Do you suppose he's going to stick around in this one long enough to find out anything about him, Ziggy?" Her antecedents were a little confused; it didn't bother her. Confusion came with the territory.

"If you'll be so good as to roll him over so my sensors can scan more efficiently, you can remove the remaining medical monitors," the disembodied voice said. The words were considerably more polite than the tone was. The woman in red gritted her teeth and did as requested. In the process she was careful to peel back both eyelids, revealing blank hazel-green eyes. A beam of red light made a swift pass before they could roll back up into his head.

"Scanning," the voice said, suddenly toneless. "EEG readings confirmed. Elimination process proceeding. Positive identification markers noted. Scanning data banks for corroboratory material initiated."

There was a pause, while the woman in red lifted with practiced skill and got her limp and unresisting patient back into the bed. It would have been nice to have help with this task, but there were security considerations. What happened here, on a regular basis, was known to very few, and she was committed to keeping it that way. She'd removed nearly all the apparatus, including IV tube and catheter, when the disembodied voice spoke again.

"Preliminary cross check through: birth reports, Selective Service records, state licensing agency records. Index check. Processing."

11

The woman in red barely heard the words. She straightened the pillow, moved an IV pole back out of the way, and twitched a sheet into position. Then, gazing down on the recumbent body, the familiar face with the single lock of white hair drooping into its eyes, she sighed. "Dear one, when is all this going to *quit*? Mamma really does want to know."

The unconscious body didn't respond.

"I have a tentative ID," the voice said.

"You better let the Admiral know," the woman in red answered. She looked back at the body again and moved her head slowly back and forth, her long earrings swaying in glittering constellations against her neck. "Here we go again," she murmured. "When you coming home, honey? When you gonna come home?"

Elsewhen, a thwarted teenage boy dragged a nauseated girl upright and shook her until her long straight hair flopped around her shoulders. "Did you see that? He threw it back in my face and took back my keg! What did he do that for?" the boy demanded.

Stifling a moan against the back of her hand, the girl shook her head, cautiously. "Ow. I dunno. Leave me alone."

"Stupid bitch, you spend enough time hanging out with him." He shoved her, and she staggered back a couple of steps and landed on her rump, staring up at him with her mouth in a round O of surprise.

A few of the others gathered around; one placed a warning hand on the boy's arm. "Better cool it, Kev. She's not your old lady any more, you can't push her around like that."

Other voices murmured agreement.

"She's not my old lady because she spends all her time with that drunk Indian who's screwing her aunt!" Kevin yelled.

"He is not!" the girl yelled back, getting to her feet. "And he isn't drunk, you are!"

12

"He's a—" Kevin began.

The girl interrupted. "He may be an Indian but he's more of a gentleman than you are!"

This was greeted with laughter and catcalls. She looked around defiantly. "Well, when was the last time Wickie beat one of you up for the fun of it? *I* think that makes him better than Kevin Hodge any day!"

Nobody wanted to answer that. Someone at the other fire found a keg that hadn't been emptied yet, and the wave of anger poised over the clearing dribbled away.

"C'mon, Kev. Let's get a drink. We don't even need the other keg." The peacemaker stumbled across the way to join the rest.

But Kevin wasn't quite ready to give up. He looked toward the opening in the trees through which the Indian had disappeared, and over to his friends—and his former girlfriend—who had seen the Indian make fun of him and get away with it, and his face contorted. "He'll be sorry," Kevin whispered. "Damn Indian."

CHAPTER
TWO

Talking sense into a crowd of drunken teens, particularly when one has just delivered the makings of the next carouse, was a waste of time and energy. Sam watched long enough to make sure the girl was going to be all right, and that no one else looked sick, and then he went up to the boy who'd paid, handed him his money back, picked up the keg, and came back the way he came. The boy came after him, shouting something about how he couldn't do that, he'd paid for it, bring it back.

Sam ignored him. The pursuit stopped when the boy fell over something behind him.

Thirty feet along his backtrack, out of sight of the fires, he found a pickup truck with a side panel emblazoned with a large white bear and the logo, "Polar Bar: Snow Owl's Finest Entertainment." The truck reeked of beer. He heaved the keg into the back end, heard it bounce and hoped it cracked, and scrambled in his pockets for keys.

He had keys. He even had a New York State driver's license, though it didn't have a picture. He got in the truck and held the license up to the overhead, studying it curiously, and compared the description to the face staring back at him from the rearview mirror.

Wickie G. W. Starczynski was twenty-two, with black hair and brown eyes. He was cleanshaven, with deepset eyes and high cheekbones and a wide, thin-lipped mouth; the reflection was dark, but Sam thought at least some of that was probably the lighting from the overhead lamp. Nobody was going to mistake him for a Celt this time around, however; the inside wrist of the hand holding the driver's license was a lightly toasted brown. He was six-two and weighed 173 pounds. He lived in a post office box.

Well, *that* was a great help.

The post office box was in Snow Owl, New York.

Maybe he'd get lucky, and find some signs.

He scrambled in the glove compartment. The truck was registered to a Rita Marie Hoffman. There was an insurance paper, with an expiration date of February 1976. It matched the expiration date on the license. Unless both this Rita Marie Hoffman and his current host were flagrantly ignoring renewals, it was sometime before February, 1976. And while it was cool, it wasn't wintertime. Early summer, maybe.

Well, that was something. Always assuming the insurance paper wasn't out of date. He knew now approximately *when* he was, and roughly *where* he was—somewhere in upstate New York. This was definitely progress.

He shifted the truck into gear and pulled out, bumping over rocks and fallen branches, wincing as branches scraped paint off the roof. He leaned back to look over his shoulder, hoping that the ruts would lead to pavement eventually.

Eventually, they did.

The seat belt was broken. After three serious tries to pull out the tongue side, he pulled it completely out of its housing.

"Great," he said, as much to hear himself talk as for any other reason.

Elsewhere, elsewhen, a parallel hybrid neurocomputer noted a glitch in reality, and began tracking a new set of rapidly branching probabilities.

He made a wild guess and pointed the truck downhill.

The road was narrow and crumbling along the edges, and there was nothing but darkness yawning on the other side of

16

the upward lane. He saw a "Beware of Falling Rocks" sign, and snorted grimly to himself.

His left headlight flickered and died, and he muttered wordlessly under his breath and slowed down even more. A gray boulder the size of a child's playhouse jutted out into his lane, and he had to cross the double yellow line to get around it.

He glanced at the odometer, as if it would tell him anything. It told him, in fact, that the Polar Bar wanted to squeeze the last possible mile out of its truck; it showed six digits plus the tenth-miles. He could feel cracks in the plastic of the steering wheel biting into his fingers, much as the nylon fibers of the rope on the balloon had.

The part of the night sky that he could see, that wasn't blocked by trees and mountains, was covered with clouds, was like velvet. He couldn't see any stars. Even if he got out of the truck and looked up, he probably wouldn't be able to find too many: maybe Orion the Hunter, with the three stars of his belt, chasing eternally after the Great Bear, but not much else.

Not like the desert. The air was clear in the desert. You could almost reach out and touch the stars. He had a sudden mental image of himself reaching up to the sky, laughing.

He blinked, and wondered where *that* memory had come from, just as a small creature bounded across the road almost under his tires, and he jammed on the brakes. The truck pulled hard to the left, toward the darkness. He jerked it back again, taking his foot off the brake, and the truck fishtailed, skidding on loose rock. The back end drifted out.

"Steer toward the skid," he muttered, not hearing himself. If he steered into the skid he'd go over the edge.

If he didn't, he'd go over the edge.

He wondered if he'd Leap before the truck hit the bottom. Of the cliff, the ravine, of whatever it was. That would leave Wickie to die, though. And he didn't think he'd Leaped into Wickie in order to trade his life for that of a squirrel.

He tapped the brakes, lightly, twisted the wheel forward, back again. The truck skidded into the soft dirt along the shoulder of the road. A chunk of granite the size of one of the truck's tires loomed up in front of him. He steered frantically for the clear space on the roadside, pumped the brakes.

The truck stopped.

Elsewhen, a new set of possibilities blinked into existence and began branching.

He took a long shuddering breath and leaned his forehead against the wheel. If he hadn't been slowing down to begin with, he would have hit that rock and flipped over.

Of course, if it hadn't been for the squirrel, he probably wouldn't have been in a skid to begin with.

"Hey, maybe next time you'll Leap into Al Unser," said an all-too-familiar gravelly voice next to him.

Sam jumped. "How long have you been there?"

"Long enough to see you miss Rocky the Flying Squirrel back there." Al shook his head. "Sam, you gotta learn about cost-benefit analysis. The benefit of hitting the nut-guzzler versus the cost of going over a very steep cliff, in this case."

"It's a good thing you didn't speak up while I was trying to straighten out. I didn't even hear you coming." Sam got out of the truck and then leaned back hastily. It was too dark to tell for sure, but it looked like the vehicle had stopped about six inches from the edge of a long drop, and this time he was positive he didn't have a bungee cord attached anywhere.

"I know that." Al's tone was distinctly injured. "You were otherwise occupied. I wasn't going to startle you. Oh," he added as an afterthought, "watch your step there. They don't have safety barriers along this road."

"I noticed." Sam swallowed his heart back into place and stomped over to the rock. It wasn't quite as big as it had looked when he was bearing down on it, but it was plenty big enough to make him grunt as he got his arms

18

around it, staggered a few feet, and heaved it over the side. The crashing and crunching as it fell went on for several seconds.

The handlink squealed loudly. Al glared at it, bushy eyebrows knit. *"Now* what, Ziggy?"

The computer Ziggy, back at Project Quantum Leap, blinked a message in the colored cubes of the handlink. Al sighed in response, the sigh of a man seeing something familiar and not particularly pleasing. His next words, however, continued the previous topic. "Besides, I didn't say anything because I was trying to get oriented. It's dark out here."

"No, really?" Sam drawled, glaring.

Al was dressed in a black shirt with interlocking vibrant yellow-pink-and-purple designs, matching suspenders, and black slacks. A black fedora with a bright blue feather in the band tilted on his head at a jaunty angle. For a change of pace, he wasn't juggling a cigar with the handlink.

"Sure it is," Al said, ignoring the sarcasm. "It's nighttime."

"It's usually dark in the nighttime. I've noticed that. Why am I here, Al?"

Why am I here, Al? One of these days he was going to ask that question and Al was going to say, *Because this is where you belong, Sam. This is home.* But he'd given up, almost, on expecting that day to come.

"Well." Al made a show of consulting the handlink. "You've Leaped into Wickie Gray Wolf Starczynski—"

"Who?" Sam interrupted, startled. "Gray Wolf?"

"Wickie Gray Wolf Starczynski. He's half–Mohawk Indian, half-Polish. Some combination, huh?"

"I guess it could be." A scrap of past history focused for him. "This isn't 1990, is it? And Canada? Didn't the Mohawks take over some place—"

"As I was saying . . . ?" Al raised one eyebrow, inviting another interruption if Sam cared to make one. Sam, recognizing Al's I'm-giving-the-briefing-here-ensign look, didn't. "It's not Canada, it's not 1990, and you're not involved in a Native American uprising." He paused, distracted momentarily. "I wonder if that should be Native Canadian? Except Ziggy says he was born in New York State, and . . . Never mind.

"It's Friday, June 6, 1975, and you're in upstate New York. You didn't pick a world-beater this time: Wickie dropped out of school in the eighth grade. He's a bartender and man-of-all-work at the Polar Bar. He was making a delivery to a private party—"

"A bunch of kids," Sam said, still annoyed. "It was a bunch of kids."

"Ahuh. So, knowing you, I gather the delivery didn't get made. That's not going to endear you to Rita Marie Hoffman, who owns the bar. Wickie lives behind the bar in one of the cabins Hoffman also owns. I suggest you not push her too far." He examined the handlink. "She has the reputation of being a feisty lady. She'll escort some drunks out of her place with a shotgun in 1978."

"What does Ziggy say I'm supposed to do this time?" Sam asked, desperately trying to bring Al back to the point.

Al chewed his lip. "We're working on it. I thought we had it. There was something about a party this coming Monday night, and preventing a wreck, but things seem to be kind of flexing at this point. Ziggy's not sure any more."

Sam sighed and looked up, past the roof of the truck cab into the side of the mountain beyond. "Why can't I ever get a straight answer?" he inquired. "Ziggy's not sure. Or there's a glitch. There's always something. Why can't I ever just Leap in, fix it, and Leap out again?"

"You've done that," Al pointed out. "You clipped the line on that balloon. If you hadn't done that, the guy would never have bounced. He'd've just gone splat."

"*I* would have gone splat, you mean, and thank you very much for letting me know!"

"What good would it have done? Of course, I didn't expect you to actually go over the side," Al said thoughtfully.

20

"Just what *were* you looking at on the handlink while I was dropping several hundred feet straight down?"

"Huh? Oh. Gooshie and I have this fantasy basketball team, and I was trying to figure out a way to buy up Michael Jordan's contract."

Sam was speechless. Al noticed. "It doesn't do any harm," he protested. "Hey, Ziggy has gigabytes of memory she doesn't use."

Sam closed his eyes and shook his head.

"Are you going to stay out here all night?" the hologram asked. "Isn't it kind of cold?" Al couldn't feel the cold. Physically, he was back in the Imaging Chamber. He couldn't touch or be touched by anything in Sam's "moment" of time. That didn't keep him from empathizing. "And they've been having thunderstorms around here. People have been seeing twisters around—" he peered at the handlink "—Ellicotville, wherever that is. And south of Rochester."

"Yeah, I guess it is pretty cold," Sam sighed. He got back into the truck, slammed the door, shifted back into gear, and edged away from the precipice, guiding the vehicle back onto the road. He drove at least two miles farther down the twisting, narrow road before the quivering in his gut calmed down.

Al, floating along in the passenger seat, kept pace. He'd found that putting a chair in the Imaging Chamber allowed it to appear to Sam that he was actually sitting in the front seat of a vehicle with him. It was better than having his body appear to be cut in half by the seat, at least.

Road signs told Sam that Snow Owl was only a mile away. He allowed himself to draw a cautious breath of relief as the road flattened out, following the bank of a stream. He passed a bowling alley, a few small houses, and then what looked like the beginnings of Snow Owl's business district. The Polar Bar was on the near end, a wooden building standing by itself. A stretch of crumbling asphalt and gravel served as a parking lot; four or five cars were nosed up to the building like puppies looking for milk.

21

The sound of a piano being beaten upon by someone with a grudge came through an open window. Neon beer signs in the windows advertised Olympia and Heineken.

"Wickie's cabin is around back," Al reminded him.

Sam hesitated, wondering whether he ought to take the keg back into the bar, and decided to avoid the inevitable confrontation for as long as possible. As Al had pointed out, the bar owner wasn't going to be happy about Wickie's failure to do his job.

Well, Sam wasn't too happy about the bar owner's customer base. Liquor to kids? It wasn't right.

A memory surfaced abruptly, a taste on his tongue, in his throat. His first beer. He'd been, what, thirteen? Tom had given it to him. It was metallic-tasting. He hadn't liked it at the time.

After a while he'd gotten used to it. He'd never really enjoyed the sensation of being drunk, though. He'd tried it once, as an experiment, in college. He kept careful notes.

He couldn't read his notes in the morning, and decided that he wasn't going to try it again.

It had never occurred to him before to wonder where or how Tom got that beer. From their father's supply, no doubt. John Beckett used to have a beer maybe once a week. It was no big deal.

He pulled around the parked cars and spotted a line of modest buildings, each perhaps a third the size of the bar, half-hidden in the trees. The one remaining headlight picked out well-used ruts that ran up to the porch of the first cabin. It seemed as likely as any of them.

He parked and got out, walked around to the back to look at the keg again. There was a tarp stuffed behind it; he pulled it out, found where it hooked up to the shell of the truck, and lashed it into place. It really wasn't good enough, but—

"Does Ziggy say anything about this keg going missing tonight?"

Al raised an eyebrow, punched an inquiry into the handlink. "Nope. It's still there in the morning."

"Good." Sam dusted off his hands and felt around in his pockets for keys to the cabin door.

There was a light on inside. Al was putting through another inquiry, a worried look on his face, when Sam swung the door open.

To see a half-dressed woman turn toward him from examining the stereo, saying, "Wickie! Baby, what took you so long?"

"Oh, *boy,*" man and hologram chorused, each with their own distinctive expression.

CHAPTER THREE

"Oh, boy," Al repeated, yearning stark in his voice. Sam would have elbowed him if it would have done any good. "But Sam, *look* at her!"

Sam was looking. He couldn't not look; the room wasn't big enough to make it convincing to look anywhere else, and besides, he was human, too. But he was a gentleman as well, and not really Wickie Gray Wolf Starczynski, and this woman wasn't talking to the person she thought she was. She'd probably be really embarrassed if she knew she was standing there, in panties and garter belt and shirt hanging open and . . . and *nothing* else, in front of a total stranger. She was an older woman, perhaps in her late forties, with graying roots beginning to show under dark auburn hair piled up high, vivid lipstick, heavy eye makeup, and scarlet toenails; she kept herself in shape. In very, very good shape indeed, in fact. The delicate smell of lilacs filled his nostrils, and he found himself taking a very deep breath, savoring the fragrance.

Al had maneuvered himself past Sam and was trying to look past the front panels of the shirt. It was a blue plaid flannel, too big for her, but it probably fit Wickie perfectly. It was draped across her breasts in such a way that Al couldn't quite see, and he raised one hand, caught sight of Sam's frankly murderous glare, and thought better of it.

"Wickie, honey, what's wrong?" The woman obviously thought the glare was meant for her. Sam made a hasty decision based on inadequate data and hoped he wasn't too far out of line. The woman had all too obviously made herself at home. He could only hope that she had another home somewhere else, too. "Aren't you glad to see me?"

"N-nothing's wrong," Sam stammered. "I just didn't expect to see you here."

"You weren't supposed to expect me. I wanted it to be a surprise. It's been *way* too long, sweetheart. Weeks, in fact. I figured it was time to do something about that."

He was reminded of the wall of heat from the burner of the hot air balloon; he could feel himself gasping for air. She licked her lips, slowly, pink tongue against dark red lipstick, ran her hand down his chest, twined her arms around his neck, pulled him closer. It would have been a parody of lust, if she weren't so obviously teasing him.

In all senses of the word.

And rather successfully, too.

Even if she *did* taste of old tobacco.

Oops.

"Oh ho," Al chortled. "Looks like you've got a fan, Sam. And a very . . . attractive one, too."

"I'm sorry, it's just—I've got a real bad headache," he said lamely, wishing he could get his hands on Al's virtual throat. "The truck—it almost went off the road—"

"What?" the woman snapped. The image of the playful seductress snapped abruptly out of existence as she stalked across the room and through Al to yank down the blinds and peer at the truck parked outside. "You know I can't afford more bills right now—Was there any damage?"

"No," Sam said, still reeling from the transition and wondering if she was going to ask about damage to Wickie, too. The most important thing appeared to be the truck, though. He didn't remember following the woman, but somehow he was standing next to her again.

"A *headache*?" Al interjected. "I haven't heard that since my second—no, my th—Come to think of it, all my wives used that line on me, one time or another. . . ."

"Who is she?" Sam mouthed behind the woman's back. Based on her reaction to the news about the truck, he had a pretty good idea, but it would be nice to get some confirmation.

"Huh? What did you say?" Al asked, belatedly realizing Sam was trying to communicate with him. Sam jabbed a finger in the woman's direction, almost catching her in the breast as she spun around; he snatched his hand back again and laughed self-consciously.

"Don't play tickle with me, dammit," she snapped. "What happened with the truck?"

"Er, nothing. It's okay, really. Really. Not a scratch on it." He winced, remembering the tree branches scraping the roof. "Well, not to speak of."

"Aw, now you got her mad," Al mourned.

She was past him, pulling the shirt off as she walked through the doorway into the next room. Sam, remaining where he was, caught a tantalizing glimpse of her back. Al followed her as if on a leash.

"*Al!*" Sam said between his teeth. The hologram paused in the doorway without looking around. "Al, will you please get back here?"

"The view is better from here," Al responded, not moving.

Sam took a very deep breath and let it out, slowly. He couldn't kill Al, though the urge was overwhelming; Al was his best friend. His buddy. His Observer, his only contact with his own life.

More to the point, Al was out of reach. "Al, will you get back here and tell me what I'm supposed to be doing here?"

"It's too late. She's getting dressed." Al sounded depressed.

"I *don't* think I'm here to make love to a total stranger," Sam said through his teeth.

27

"Since when am I a total stranger?" the woman snapped, reentering the room by walking through the hologram. She was fully dressed now, wearing sandals, flowery bell-bottom pants, and a short, rib-hugging top to match. "And you better believe, if there's any damage to that truck, it's coming out of your paycheck." She marched past Sam and out the door.

Paycheck? It had to be Rita Marie Hoffman. Sam watched her examine the sides and fenders, and hoped she wouldn't raise the tarp. He didn't think she'd be happy about finding a full quarter-keg back there.

Fortunately she didn't find enough damage to send her back into the cabin, looking for blood. She glanced back once at the bewildered man standing in the light of the doorway and made a disgusted gesture and marched off. Sam breathed a sigh of relief and made a mental note to see if he could get that headlight replaced before she found out about it.

"Another one of life's great lost opportunities," Al mourned.

"Do you suppose you could rein in your libido just long enough to find me some information about this Leap?" Sam asked, dripping sarcasm. "For starters, who was that woman?" It never hurt to verify his data.

"Another one of life's great lost opportunities," Al repeated. "Sam, how do you do it? Leap after Leap? All these women, throwing themselves at you, and you just . . . you just . . . ." He was practically in tears.

"Al, is Tina on vacation or something?" Sam asked.

"How did you know?" Al asked, his eyes glittering suspiciously.

"You're just being a little more Al than usual, that's all. Look, she's gone now. Would you mind coming back to earth long enough to find out what I'm supposed to be doing here? Or is that too much to ask?"

"What? Oh, yeah." The focus of his distraction having left his direct line of vision, Al managed to pull himself together long enough to look at the handlink. He had to wipe the sweat off before he could read the pattern of blinking lights.

"Uh-hmmm." He cast a furtive glance at Sam. Sam folded his arms and waited, none too patiently. "Well. It seems there's a ninety-eight-percent chance that your visitor was Rimae—er, Rita Marie Hoffman, the lady who owns the bar. I guess they call her Rimae. There's a *ninety-nine-percent* chance that she's having a—uh—relationship with Wickie."

"I'd say so," Sam agreed dryly. "Unfortunately, I'm not Wickie."

"But you *could* be," Al began. Sam raised his eyebrows. "Oh, all right. Ziggy says he hasn't quite figured out what you're supposed to change."

"What about those kids up the mountain?" Sam suggested. "Does Ziggy know anything about them?"

"Hey, there's an idea." Al tapped in a series of codes. "Ouch. Not good."

"What is it?"

Al pursed his lips. "Well, during the ski season most of those kids spend their free time working at the slopes. But in the summertime, there isn't much going on in Snow Owl, so—"

"So they get together out on the mountain and they drink."

"And they drink," Al said. He paused. Al knew quite a bit about drinking for entertainment, and what the consequences could be. Sam thought the Observer could probably see a lot of himself in the restless teenagers.

"So what else should I know?"

Al drew in a deep breath and let it out again. "Wickie's the bartender at the Polar Bar—"

"You told me that already. Unfortunately, I don't know anything about bartending."

"I could probably help you out on that. Anyway, he's the bartender. He's been here for the last couple of years. He does odd jobs for the boss lady." He raised one eyebrow

29

meaningfully. Sam groaned and started taking off his shirt, flexing the shoulder he'd carried the keg on and rubbing at the sore spot.

If he ever got home again, Sam promised himself, Al Calavicci was going to pay for a lot of things. The process of Leaping knocked random holes in an otherwise photographic memory; he depended on Al for information about large chunks of his own past, varying from Leap to Leap. But if there was any justice in the universe at all, his Swiss-cheesed memory would let him remember all the times Al, who liked to pretend that he had the morals of the average goat, had gleefully tormented him about his encounters with women who thought they were dealing with husbands and lovers, not a time-lost quantum physicist caught in an experiment gone, as Al had once put it, "a little ca-ca."

"Could we get back to business, please?" he said through gritted teeth.

He could have sworn that bushy eyebrow couldn't possibly get any higher. That would teach him to swear, no doubt. "If you *don't* mind . . ." he emphasized, rotating his right arm.

"Well, depends on the business, I guess, but since the lady has left . . ." Al sighed. "Ziggy says"—the Observer cocked an eyebrow at the handlink—"there's a forty-three-percent chance Wickie's gonna get fired in the next few days." He cast an appraising eye over Sam, now stripped to his briefs and going through some stretching exercises in an effort to loosen up tight muscles. "For non-performance of duty, the data says."

He was going to hang Al Calavicci from the highest yard-arm, Sam promised himself. If the Navy wouldn't loan him a yardarm, he'd build one himself. He continued the stretches, not giving the hologram the satisfaction of a response. It was a good thing Wickie was in good shape; the kinks came out pretty easily. On the other hand, it was taking some effort to work up a sweat.

It was taking a *lot* of effort to ignore the smell of lilacs still lingering in the air, and the memory of the woman standing there, with the shirt hanging open. He pushed himself harder.

"But you—or Wickie, anyway—continue to stay in Snow Owl. So you must still be performing *some* duties," Al went on, all cherubic innocence. Sam gritted his teeth and reached up to put his palms flat against the ceiling.

"Let me guess," he said. "Ziggy doesn't really have the slightest idea what I'm supposed to be doing here. Forty-three percent is practically nothing."

"Nope, Ziggy has no idea. But *I* do."

"Enough already, Al. Knock it off. I know what you think, and I'm really not interested. Give me the background, okay?"

Al conceded, and adopting a much more businesslike tone, continued, "Rita—Rimac—Hoffman's been divorced seventeen years. She's got an adopted son, Davey, nineteen, who works in the bar. He's mildly retarded. And a niece, Bethica, just turned eighteen—Ziggy says Bethica's the one who was involved in the wreck that may or may not happen on Monday, by the way. Bethica is Rimae's brother's daughter. Her parents died when she was three—she's lived with Rimae ever since.

"Rimac's had it rough, but she owns the bar free and clear, and she's pretty well respected in Snow Owl."

"And Wickie?" Now he was down on the wide-planked floor, doing abdominal crunches.

"I already told you almost all of it. He's got an eighth-grade education, has worked a few dozen places. Got thrown into jail a few years ago for drunk and disorderly, but they didn't press charges. Clean record otherwise. Ziggy can't find much on him. He doesn't go anywhere or do anything with his life, as far as we can see. Never gets married. Dies of exposure in one of the big snowstorms of 1994."

"Well," Sam muttered, beginning to pant, "we've had less to go on."

31

"Aren't there splinters down there?" Al said, distracted from the handlink by the sight of Wickie—Sam—curling and uncurling his body in precise rhythm. Sam Beckett had kept himself fit with a variety of martial arts exercises. Wickie might not do sabbatt or mu tai or karate, but he was in good shape nonetheless.

"Haven't found any yet," Sam grunted. Sweat was beginning to trickle down the midline of his chest.

"I always used a cold shower, myself," Al said to nobody in particular. "Different strokes, I guess."

"Am I going to have to put up with this for this whole Leap?" Sam demanded, staring up from the floor. His fingers were still laced behind his head, his arms flat on the floor. His chest rose and fell as he panted from the exertion.

"Put up with what?"

"I thought you had a backup girlfriend for when Tina was on vacation."

"Me?" Al was the picture of injured innocence. "I wouldn't cheat on Tina. Not since that time she caught me with Nancy—or maybe Terri—no, it was Carlotta, and—"

"Who's Carlotta? I thought it was Desiree. Monica? Maria? Annie?—Never mind, I don't want to know." The number and variety of Al's backup girlfriends was legendary.

"You'll never know how much you're missing." Al grinned reminiscently.

"I hope not."

"Not if you're going to insist on being so damn pure all the time."

"Yeah, but think of all the things I don't have to worry about. STDs, AIDS, unplanned pregnancies . . . "

"You don't have to worry about those things anyway if you look at it as an exercise in logistics. I've never had a single problem." He paused. "Or a married one either."

"Al." Now Sam's arms were over his eyes. "Al, please, go away, go make up with Tina, go find Carlotta, Terri,

32

Nancy, all of them! I don't care. But don't come back until you're rational again."

"Well, if you're going to be that way about it. I could probably find somebody if I really wanted to." Al punched in the code, stepped backward, and the Door slid down.

And Al was gone. The room was blessedly silent, except for the sound of Sam's own ragged breathing. He had a stitch in his side, and he waited for it to fade out before he sat up and continued the movement to end standing again.

He needed a shower. The logical place for the shower was on the other side of the door Rita had been on, and he stuck his head around the frame carefully, feeling a little foolish but wanting to make sure the room really was empty, first. It was a good thing the room *was* empty. What would the occupant have thought, hearing only Sam's half of the recent conversation? It was enough to boggle the mind. Usually he was more careful than that.

Wickie wasn't the neatest housekeeper in the world, but he wasn't a complete slob either, Sam was relieved to find. The bed was more or less made, and the sheets looked as if they'd been changed recently. A pair of jeans draped over the back of a chair, and the top right-hand drawer of the dresser stood a couple of inches open. More jeans hung in the closet; the bottom dresser drawer held a supply of T-shirts.

If he ever got home again, he had a great career in front of himself as a burglar, he thought. After too many years of practice, he could go through someone's possessions in twenty minutes flat and tell whether he or she was married, had kids, where the occupant went to school, and what their favorite flavor of Jell-O was. Wickie wasn't married, didn't have kids, and didn't eat Jell-O. As for going to school, Sam found an elementary algebra book on the counter in the kitchen, with pencil marks in the margins. Two other books, both westerns, and six magazines constituted the remainder of the reading material in the cabin. Four of the magazines, hidden under the sofa, featured hyperdeveloped

33

mammary glands. Sam was glad his Observer wasn't around to critique them. At least Wickie had the excuse of being only twenty-two.

The bathroom showed signs that Rimae had made herself at home; he was fairly sure the still-wet, delicately scented lilac soap, the slender pink razor, and the loofah sponge weren't Wickie's. Besides, there was a second razor available, and another bar of soap, which he made grateful use of.

Twenty minutes later he was feeling much better, much more self-possessed. But the clock on the dresser said it was two-thirty in the morning, and there was nothing left to do but go to bed.

CHAPTER

FOUR

Time at the Project didn't always match Sam's. It might be noon wherever Sam was and midnight at the Project. In this case, Al had returned to the Imaging Chamber and decided he had time to go to his office and work for a few hours. Now he was wishing he'd found some other way to put things off. The administration offices were empty. The only sounds were from the environmental controls and that annoying hum from the light bulb down the hall that was almost burned out.

Another maintenance request to sign off on.

Al Calavicci had read one too many maintenance reports, recalculated one too many salary increase budgets, offered one too many testimonies before committees which would never see the light of the Congressional Record. He was fed up with administration. He was fed up with Total Quality Management. He was fed up with the Project. He was staring at the latest set of federal requirements for management of stress reduction in the workplace and thinking seriously about quitting.

Too often, these days, he had to remind himself that they were trying to bring Sam Beckett back. If it weren't for the fact that he was the only one who could contact Sam, he would have resigned long since, sick of watching hundreds of people batter themselves senseless against a puzzle that simply would not be cracked. If it weren't for the fact that Sam was still out there—

And it was getting harder and harder to measure the cost of continuing the Project against the difficulty of convincing the Project's sponsors that while the shell of Sam Beckett, Ph.D., Ph.D., Ph.D., Ph.D., Ph.D., Ph.D., M.D., was still in the Waiting Room, what occupied that shell was *not* Sam Beckett, that God or Time, Fate or whatever had thrown him back in the past to put things right that had gone wrong.

It had been a lot easier to convince them when the bill was only nine or ten billion. Now they were beginning to question whether Sam had ever really disappeared at all. "Look at his fingerprints," they argued. "Those are Dr. Beckett's. The retinal imprints are the same. The DNA is the same. How can you say Sam Beckett is missing?"

The only physical evidence was in the brain scans. Once the difference was pointed out to them, even congressional aides could see the difference between Sam Beckett's ultraencephalograph patterns and those of X2 test pilot Captain Tom Stratton; of private detective Nick Allen; of Jimmy La Matta, who had Down's syndrome; of Cheree Walters, teenage singer; of secretary Samantha Stormer; of any of the dozens of people he'd Leaped into in the past several years. But now the people controlling funding were muttering about forgeries, about substitutions, about outright fraud. There were suggestions that Sam had completely lost touch with reality, that the whole Project was involved in a conspiracy to protect their Director and prevent him from (a) obtaining the psychiatric help he so desperately needed or (b) being exposed as a hopeless paranoid schizophrenic. Not that they believed any of it, but it would make an excellent excuse to shut things down, to make a cut in the deficit. Ever since Congress had pulled the plug on the Superconducting Supercollider, they'd had it in for basic science.

Al snorted softly.

The best witness, and sometimes the only defense that made any difference, was Ziggy. They bargained for time to keep searching for a solution by renting out Ziggy's problem-solving capabilities, with Al acting as the front man and chief salesperson for the Project's computational capabilities. But Ziggy was more than just an incredibly advanced computer; it was self-aware, and it made its own bargains. It agreed to work on the calculations for traffic control in the Greater Los Angeles Metropolitan area, the balancing of the declining water table for the San Fernando Valley, seven or eight major sports books for Las Vegas casinos, stress-reduction studies, the Human Genome Project, and flood-control calculations nationwide for the U.S. Army Corps of Engineers, if and *only* if it was allowed to continue the search for the secret of Sam Beckett's return undisturbed. Al might tell Sam he was playing fantasy basketball; actually, Ziggy had been calculating the effect of certain minor tectonic shifts on the New Madrid fault.

It was discreet blackmail, was what it was, and Al Calavicci was never sure whether the Project was the blackmailer or the blackmailee. At least he had the comfort of knowing that the government didn't realize the consequences, the ramifications of a random factor in the past. They were satisfied, at least for the time being, with the tidbits Ziggy offered, and for the most part left the Project alone, never realizing the desperate focus of its work.

But it never seemed to do any good. They never seemed to make any progress. Since the day in 1995 when Sam Beckett stepped into the Accelerator, determined to prove his theory was right, they seemed to be caught in an endless loop: Sam Leaped, made some minor change in history, and Leaped, and made some minor change in history, and Leaped, and made some minor change . . . but never came home. None of the solutions offered, none of the measures attempted, ever seemed to have an effect.

They were no closer to bringing him home than they were that first day, when the body of Sam Beckett had collapsed in the Imaging Chamber and Ziggy told them what had happened. Meanwhile, the past was getting more and more confusing.

Al sighed and propped his feet up on the corner of his desk, surreptitiously unwrapping a long cigar and wadding the plastic into a ball between his fingers. It was against federal regulations to smoke anywhere within a public building; since federal funds built the Project, his office qualified as "public," even though it was necessary to add several sigmas to a Q clearance to get in. Nothing said he couldn't stick an unlighted stogie in his mouth, though.

It was a neat, well-organized room, with space on the wall for a shadow box holding assorted medals and honors and an American flag, a presentation from his retirement more than a dozen years before. The desk was metal, standard-issue gunmetal gray, though he could have requisitioned a wooden desk with a glossy sheen; he wanted something he could work on and put his feet on and kick from time to time, so he stuck to metal, and if visitors thought it was less than he was entitled to, that was their problem, not his. *He* knew who he was.

A wide strip of graph paper ran the length of one wall, with a series of dates plotted against each other, zigging and zagging insanely in lines of blue and red. Only Al and Ziggy knew what the dates stood for; there was no discernible pattern. If there had been, Ziggy would have told him; the graph paper was there as a concession to human frailty, a visual representation of the incidence and duration of Sam's Leaps. The gaps between Leaps were a mystery still. They had no idea where Sam was during the interLeap, or why weeks could go by at the Project when, to Sam, no time at all had passed from one crisis to the next.

Stress reduction. Like the stress of stepping out of the Imaging Chamber, into—Al took a deep breath. He didn't even want to think about it. Al wondered if the studies Ziggy was working on addressed a stress situation like *this*. He doubted it.

These days he had to make himself go down to the Waiting Room to greet each new stranger. He'd seen so many. Sam had been every color, every sex, every level of intelligence—

Well, no, come to think of it, no, he hadn't. Because what Leaped was still, always, essentially Sam Beckett. So while he might occupy, for instance, the body of a retarded man, somehow Sam Beckett's mind managed to use the sometimes inadequate organic equipment and yet remain Sam Beckett. Al's eyes narrowed.

"Ziggy, could that be why his memory Swiss-cheeses?" he said to the empty air.

"Could *what* be, Admiral?" The voice responding out of the still-empty air was a woman's, light and beautiful and faintly peevish. "I can't read your mind, you know."

Al hiked an eyebrow. He wasn't sure he believed that last remark. "Could Sam's memory be affected by his occupying other brains?"

"Yes," the reply came, without hesitation.

Al waited. He could hear nothing but the subdued roar of the air-conditioning system and, off in the distance from the cubicles outside his office, a ringing telephone. "Well?" he prompted at last.

"Well, what?" The voice was definitely petulant by now. "It's certainly a viable hypothesis, Admiral, but there's no way to test it, and certainly no way to run a controlled experiment. *I* don't understand the human soul, or mind, or whatever it is. Not any more than I understand God or Fate or Chance or Time or Whatever. I'm *only* a computer, after all."

If Ziggy were a flesh-and-blood woman, Al would be budgeting perfume at this point; the computer sounded like his third ex-wife, those times she claimed he wasn't paying her enough attention.

But Ziggy wasn't flesh and blood, exactly. She was neural tissue and electronic circuits and one hell of an ego. Al

39

wondered whether that ego was supposed to be a result of *his* contribution to the neural chips. He didn't think so. Sam had done that part of the programming, with Gooshie's help. And it sure wasn't Gooshie's ego; the poor guy didn't have any to spare.

Which left Sam. Sam Beckett, egomaniac.

Naaah. Al chomped on the cigar. "Well, I thought if anybody could figure it out, it was you."

"It won't solve the problem of bringing him home."

Al sighed. "Nothing's gonna bring him home," he muttered.

"That's not true!" Ziggy said sharply. "We *will* bring him home! It may take time—"

"It's already taken ten years. If the most advanced computer on earth can't figure out what went wrong in ten years of calculations, nobody can. We're all going to be dead first."

"Admiral!"

Al thought he could hear shock and, yes, fear in the computer's voice. Perversely, he continued. "Well, look at the odds. Figure your own probabilities—that seems to be your favorite thing to do. How many times has he almost died? Do you really think you're going to get it figured out before he manages to get himself killed? Every single Leap it's the same thing."

The silence was eons long, for a computer.

"I can only conjecture," Ziggy said at last, much subdued, "that whatever it is that controls Dr. Beckett's Leaps wouldn't permit him to die."

"You want to take a chance?" Al challenged. He shouldn't enjoy torturing the poor computer so much, he knew, but he could say these things only to Ziggy, and he had to say them, sometimes, to somebody. "If you're so sure Somebody Up There is taking care of him—if it would save him somehow—how about we let him go through a whole Leap sometime and let him wing it? See if miracles really do happen?"

"I won't abandon him," Ziggy said quietly. Al bit his lip, ashamed of himself.

"I wouldn't ei——" he started, when the computer interrupted.

"It's also true," Ziggy said thoughtfully, "that if we accept the possibility that some outside intelligence is directing the Leaps for a purpose, then we must also accept that this intelligence has chosen Dr. Beckett as its instrument because it is unable to intervene directly. And if that's the case, that intelligence would be unable to protect Dr. Beckett in a life-threatening situation. And the question of whether that intelligence would permit him to die is moot, since it cannot prevent his death, any more than it can intervene directly to effect the changes it wishes to make.

"I'm aware that I can have no contact with Dr. Beckett without you, Admiral, but I repeat: I will not abandon him."

Al tossed the file onto the stack on the table. "Oh hell, Ziggy, neither will I. I'm just frustrated."

There was a long companionable silence, and then the computer speakers released a long sound that was Ziggy's version of a sigh.

"Go get some sleep, Admiral," the computer said. "It's late."

Al looked around the office, at the stacks of papers, the never-ending piles of reports and notices. "I never really appreciated a good yeoman before," he muttered. Getting up, he shoved the nearest pile of paper lopsided. He liked things neat and tidy; you didn't go to sea and have things lying around loose. If a storm came up, things could get broken or lost.

But there were times when things were so screwed up anyway that it didn't much matter. Like now. This time they were a *real* mess.

"Admiral," Ziggy said again, with unwonted patience. "Mrs. Calavicci is waiting."

CHAPTER
FIVE

Wickie woke up again fully dressed, lying on an examining table set up in a corner of the white room. The woman in the red dashiki sat primly a few feet away, her hands resting lightly on her knees. She looked tired, as if she was at the end of a long day that wouldn't stop.

"Welcome, Mr. Starczynski."

He expected a hangover, or at least some kind of headache, after being drugged. But his mind was clear, and he actually felt pretty good, considering. He sat up smoothly and looked down at himself. Shirt and pants; a different style from the one he was used to, but the colors, brown and green, were agreeable. He wore soft slippers instead of shoes. That told him he wasn't expected to go anywhere. But the place didn't stink like jail, and it didn't look like jail, either.

He took a long appraising look around.

Over at the other end of the room, past the single door, was the bed, the machinery, the stairs, the observation deck—all the things he'd seen before he'd been gassed to sleep. Opposite him was the woman. There was no one else in the room.

He looked at her and waited, patient and suspicious. She bore his gaze with equanimity. If he tried anything, he guessed, they'd just gas him again. And even if he could get out of here, where would he go?

"My name is Dr. Verbeena Beeks," she said. "You're probably wondering what's happened to you."

He snorted softly to himself, kept his face impassive.

She waited to see if he'd ask any questions. When he kept quiet, she went on.

"The first thing is, we're really sorry you're here. You have no *idea* how sorry." She drew in a breath. She couldn't possibly sit up any straighter. She looked like a picture in one of Bethica's books, a picture of a queen of some place in Africa. "You've accidentally become involved in an experiment that's gone wrong. It's our sincere hope that very shortly you'll return to your proper place. It would help us if you'd tell us everything you can about yourself and the people you know."

Wickie thought about this. Experiment? That sounded like the government. She was holding something back, of course. There was more to the story. He looked down at his hands, clutching the edge of the examining table, and he didn't recognize them at all.

He wondered how much she wasn't telling him, and decided to see if he could find out. "What kind of experiment?"

"It's an experiment in quantum physics," she said.

Uncertainty. She wasn't all that sure about this part herself. But physics, that was government, for sure.

"The result is that you've . . . switched places . . . with one of our people. He has to take certain actions. Once he does, you'll switch back, and you probably won't remember anything about this." She wasn't sure about that, either, he could tell.

Switched places. He lifted his right hand, rotated it, examined it. It was too pale, and there wasn't any scar across the heel of his hand.

Not his hand.

Switched places.

Demons stole people's souls, his mother had told him. They came in the night, creatures with twisted faces, and

44

they took people away and they were never seen again. He never really believed that stuff. This black woman, she didn't look like a demon. This place didn't look like any version of Hell he'd ever heard about.

Still. Not his hand. Witchcraft.

He clenched "his" fist, watching fascinated as the hand that was not his hand moved and tightened. It *felt* like his hand felt—strong, the muscles moving and shifting; the nails biting into the palm brought the same edged pain. But *his* hands weren't so big, so white. He suppressed a shudder of panic. He wouldn't let this woman see him be afraid.

She'd said something about switching back, if—He had to have more information. He had to. Not really expecting an answer, he asked, "What actions?"

Abruptly, she looked exasperated and much more human. "I *don't know*. Nobody knows. We're trying to figure that out. That's why we need information from you."

"Well, if you don't know what actions, how do you know I'll—switch back with this guy?" He was pushing it hard, he knew. He had no reason to think a government person would tell him anything. Government people liked to say things and act superior and they didn't like questions. But this woman was answering him so far.

She slumped, just the tiniest bit. Definitely not a demon, then; he couldn't remember any stories where demons looked sad. "Because that's the way it's always worked before."

The past was no guarantee of the future. On the other hand, he didn't have anything better to go on, and it looked like this doctor woman didn't either. "This happens a lot, then?"

Dr. Beeks nodded, biting her lip. Demons didn't do that, either.

"And it always switches back okay?"

She opened her mouth to say something, then stopped. He watched with interest, waiting for the signs that she was going to lie to him.

The signs didn't come. "Once a man switched back in

time to die," she said. "We can't control that. But mostly everything goes back okay. Better than it was before."

He looked back down at his pale hand. Switching back was better?

Better than being stuck behind a bar, watching the white kids reach for what he'd never had?

The black woman had said so.

And it was better to be yourself, always. His mother had told him that, back when he was young and foolish and wondered who he really was, when his cousins on each side of the family made fun of him for being part of the other.

He raised the unfamiliar hand. "Who is this man?"

She hesitated. Now the lies would come. But instead, she said, "I'm sorry. I can't tell you that, because if we succeed in switching you back, we can't let you remember any of this."

He grinned then, a tight unpleasant grin. "Afraid I might go looking for him and punch him out, huh?"

She laughed. "Well, you might. Even though it isn't his fault either. He's caught, just like you are."

Caught. Trapped in *his*, Wickie Gray Wolf's, body. He felt a flare of anger. How dare this white man take his body from him?

At least she was being honest with him. So far.

"What do you want to know?" he asked cautiously.

They weren't his quarters, for one thing. And the woman waiting for him, the woman Ziggy called "Mrs. Calavicci"—he never thought he'd get married again without Sam to stand up for him. If Sam stood up for him the marriage would last, he'd always believed. A walking good-luck charm, that was Sam Beckett.

And the terrifying part was, he didn't even know who she *was*.

He'd cut the connection with Sam and the first thing Ziggy said, before Al even had a chance to ask, was, "Admiral, you're married in this present." He'd stood there in the

46

Imaging Chamber, surrounded by blank walls, gasping like a gaffed fish, his mouth opening and closing, completely unable to react.

Sam's Leaping changed things; he'd gotten used to that. Once, on a trip to Washington, he'd been testifying before a congressional committee and watched the chairman change to a chairwoman before his very eyes. Nobody else had noticed; he'd slipped without missing a beat into a different future created by Sam's actions in the past.

But the past Sam was in now had thrown up a new future, like flotsam onto the beach, that Al Calavicci was supposed to live in. Be a *part* of.

He wondered briefly what would happen if Sam changed something so that he, Al, wasn't part of the Project. Would he know? Would he even realize anything had happened?

Probably not. He wouldn't even remember anything had ever been different.

He was stalling. He could tell he was stalling.

He'd never heard of this woman, this "Janna" before, never seen her, and he was supposed to walk in and be a loving husband. It scared him more than he wanted to admit.

She had to be connected with the Project somehow, he knew that much; this was not a place where people brought their families, raised kids, and built computers to sell commercially. A scientist, an engineer, an administrator, a janitor?

If he really concentrated, he *might* be able to remember her—one face out of a couple of thousand faces that made up the workers on the Project.

A personnel specialist, Ziggy said. With a specialty in counseling. In this history Al had met Janna Fulkes in 1993, and married her last year. She wasn't his usual type, but they'd been happy together, Ziggy said.

Al had beaten a strategic retreat to his office, unable to cope. He buried himself in paperwork and tried not to wonder about "not your usual type."

Happy. That was good to know, as he stood now in front of a door to quarters he'd never seen before, prepared to enter a life he didn't know. He closed his eyes and smothered a wry chuckle. Sam Beckett wasn't the only one who leaped into his own life.

Raising his hand to knock on the door, he paused. He lived here. He ought to just walk in . . . .

The quarters were larger than the ones he thought of as his own. He stood in the entryway, looking around.

Unlike the Spartan place he thought of as his own, these rooms looked as if people lived here. Before him was a cozy living room with a blue camelback sofa, a wood-and-glass coffee table, a couple of easy chairs, with an HDTV and sound system along one wall. On the coffee table were a couple of magazines and a reproduction Chinese jade horse—at least he hoped it was reproduction. If it wasn't, he was a lot poorer than he'd been this morning.

The far wall was covered with the various plaques, commendations, and commemorations of years of Navy service, and family pictures.

Wedding pictures. Of himself. With a smiling woman.

If he closed his eyes, and concentrated—and it was taking less and less concentration as the minutes ticked by—he could *remember* that wedding picture being taken. He swallowed dryly.

He could remember a whole series of things, things that never happened. Meeting Janna. Making a token pass—he hadn't been that interested in her, really, but it was expected of him. And she'd laughed at him.

He shook himself. None of this had ever happened. None of it. He denied it. He wasn't married. He'd never met anyone named Janna. He'd stepped into the Imaging Chamber a happily randy single man with five marriages behind him, and stepped out again married, and somehow he could almost remember both pasts, as if they were both real. The memories shifted in and out of focus. At one moment, he knew he was involved with Tina, was determinedly single

48

after five marriages. At the next, he knew just as certainly that he had met and romanced and married Janna, that Tina had never been a factor in his life. The memories blurred in places, stood sharp in others. It was as if Sam's Swiss-cheese effect had reached out and affected him, too. But that wasn't possible.

Then who was the woman coming out of the back room, dressed in blue jeans and an ivory lace blouse, smiling at him?

"Al, honey. How's it going—" She paused, looked at him with concern. "Is something wrong? Is Sam all right?"

She was only an inch or so taller than he was, and at least twenty years younger. She was slender and graceful and moved lightly, like a dancer. Her brown hair was medium length. Her eyes were blue.

She looked too damned much like Beth. He gasped for air, for balance.

Instantly she was at his side, holding the back of her hand against his forehead, loosening his tie. "Al? What's wrong? Is it your heart?"

His *heart*? He bit back an imprecation, "remembering" just in time that references to his poor, weak heart were a running joke between the two of them, a way of acknowledging the age difference and defusing it as an issue. It was always the first thing she asked if he looked sick. Besides, the back of her hand felt wonderfully cool on his forehead, and her lips were wonderfully soft in a greeting kiss.

And she *was* his wife, after all. So he responded.

He seemed to have retained some habits from his other past lifetime. Of course, it never hurt when his partner was as enthusiastic as this. He was beginning to get thoroughly involved when she whispered in his ear, "Tina's coming by in a few minutes . . . ."

Tina?

"Tina, uh, Martinez-O'Farrell?"

Janna drew back and looked him in the eyes. "Of course Tina Martinez-O'Farrell, who else? She had some extension plans she wanted to run past you. Al, what's wrong? Something's bothering you, I can tell."

"Well, you were doing a pretty good job of bothering me a minute ago," he said hoarsely. Tina? Here? He used to have nightmares about two or more girlfriends cornering him at the same time.

Well, okay, sometimes they weren't nightmares. But this time wasn't likely to be one of *those*. He didn't have girlfriends now, he was almost certain.

"Not that, silly." She slapped him lightly on his bare chest, revealed through the disarray of an unbuttoned shirt. "Come on, what is it? You don't usually give me the tiger treatment after a long day at the office."

"I must be slipping."

"Albert." Unlike certain of his previous wives—Al wondered suddenly how many previous wives he'd had in this particular timeline—her use of his name indicated great patience and a certain amount of humor, along with the more standard "time to quit the fancy footwork, Calavicci."

He closed his eyes and shook his head. "It's nothing, really." The mood was completely ruined; he started rebuttoning, as much to give himself something to do as anything else. How was he supposed to explain to her that he almost/not quite/sort of remembered who she was? She wasn't even one of the crowd of willing stand-ins Sam had charged him with only hours earlier. Except for those almost-memories, she was as much a stranger to him as Rita Marie Hoffman was to Sam, and whether he liked it or not he understood Sam's position all too well.

If he were Sam Beckett, pernicious honesty would demand that he try explaining, just as Sam would've to Rita Marie if the "rules" of quantum leaping had allowed him to. He wasn't Sam Beckett, and he had learned the first rule of the military about the time this woman was born. Never volunteer. Never, never, never volunteer.

It occurred to him, of a sudden, that he could probably resolve this mess simply by taking the handlink and going back into the Imaging Chamber and encouraging Sam to do something. Anything. Lord only knew what small things would change the future. A dead butterfly in the Cretaceous could lead to a new world government; doubtless Sam Beckett's choice of breakfast beverage could get Al Calavicci out of an unexpected marriage . . . .

Janna smiled at him.

Well. He didn't have to change things right away, did he? It could always wait until morning. Couldn't it?

SATURDAY

June 7, 1975

Poor intricated soul! Riddling, perplexed, laby-
rinthical soul!

—John Donne, Sermon XLVIII

CHAPTER
SIX

People who believed in reincarnation, Sam had noticed, always thought their past lives were special, that they'd been kings or queens or famous in some way. It really wasn't fair. All *his* lives seemed to come down to pushing a broom.

He shoved a chair back out of the way to scrape crumbled corn chips from under the table. The bar area was spotless, speaking well for whoever had covered for Wickie the night before, but the tables were a mess. He thought you were supposed to reverse the chairs and put them up on the table when you closed a bar for the night; evidently that piece of folk wisdom wasn't universal.

He straightened up and counted. Thirty tables, plus the booths against the back wall, and the benches by the fireplace. It was a nice fireplace—fieldstone, with a wide mantel. Wouldn't hold more than a couple oxen. Or maybe three or four of those elk whose heads decorated the wall, or a half dozen of the buck. But the stone was clean, shades of pale yellow and gray and pink. He doubted it had ever been used for anything at all. The stone hearth was spotless, and the broom and shovel and brass fire iron looked as if they'd been purchased only yesterday. It was a shame, really. He liked a nice fire in a fireplace.

Then there was the Bar. Or B'ar. The polar bear that

gave the bar its name towered eight feet tall on its hind legs, mouth agape, front legs pawing at the air with claws like curved black knives, was actually more yellow than strictly white, but it had certainly been alive once upon a time. Unlike the fireplace, it was far from pristine; a little motheaten, in fact, when one inspected it closely.

On the other side of the fireplace stood a baby grand piano, probably the one he'd heard pounded on the night before, and he couldn't resist running a few scales; it was even in tune. He hoped he'd get the chance to really play before he Leaped out. He missed music.

No one else was up at this hour. He'd awakened at sunrise, gotten up and dressed, and looked around for something to eat. Wickie leaned to cereal with skim milk and cinnamon-raisin bagels with cream cheese and orange juice, which was fine with Sam.

After breakfast he had retrieved the keys and checked out the truck. The damage didn't seem too bad in the harsh light of day; he thought he could probably replace the burned-out headlamp himself if Wickie had the right tools. From there he'd wandered over to the bar. One of the keys fit the back door, so he'd gone in. The place was enough of a mess that he'd grabbed a broom to keep himself busy until he had a better idea of what he was supposed to do next.

Lacking further direction, he found a broom and bucket and a mop and some cleaner, and started on the floor, scraping up the detritus of dead cigarette butts, smashed pretzels, and wide sticky patches of beer spills.

Once the floor was reasonably clean, he emptied out the bucket in the sink in the utility closet and paused. Tables, he thought; he didn't know how Wickie felt about it, but he decided he'd draw the line at cleaning bathrooms if at all possible. He started on the tables.

It was kind of nice, actually. Nobody around, no hassles, no life-threatening crises. Not even Al. Well, he kind of missed Al, but he never seemed to have much time all by himself to think about things.

When he thought about things, his thoughts invariably ended up, eventually, at the same place. Home.

It had been so long since he'd been home he'd almost forgotten what it was like. He couldn't remember it very well: scraps and bits and pieces of pictures, scenes; sharp, clear images of people without names.

He knew what his mother looked like, because the vagaries of his Swiss-cheese memory hadn't shot a hole into that particular image—not yet, not this time, anyway. He had no idea any more what his sister Katie looked like as an adult, though he could remember her as a child. He thought his brother Tom was alive, but he didn't want to ask, in case he was wrong, in case something else had happened after the Leap in which he had changed things so Tom didn't die in Vietnam.

He could remember, as if reading them off the page, most of the equations supporting the theory of quantum leaping. He still didn't know what had gone wrong. According to Al, nobody back at the Project quite knew, either. He couldn't remember what the Project was like, though he knew Gooshie had bad breath and Tina had red hair.

He probably knew that from Al, though.

There had to be lots of other people there, but he couldn't remember them.

He sighed and finished polishing the last table. There were always windows to do. The Polar Bar featured stained-glass panels with large panes of red and gold and blue and green, underneath clerestory windows of clear glass. Sunlight made colored jewels of light across the floors and tables and the bar. The door was paneled in oak and heavy, mottled amber glass. It gave the place a vaguely men's-club feeling, dark and burrowsome with occasional glimmers of beauty.

Someone rattled at the front door. He put the rag aside. He could see only a vague shadow through the glass, so he cracked the door open an inch or so. "Yes?"

It was the angry kid from the night before, and he shoved

the door open, pushing Sam aside. He had medium brown hair and dark brown eyes that glittered with anger. His pupils were too small, Sam noted with a clinical part of his mind—some chemical influence there. The boy's fingers, curled around the door frame, were white and yellow with pressure.

"I want to know what the hell you thought you were doing last night!" the kid demanded, his voice cracking.

"There's a law about serving liquor to minors," Sam said mildly, moving just in time to block his visitor from actually entering. He didn't think the kid was stupid enough to start anything, but just in case, it was always a good idea to keep him on the other side of the portal. At least the frame would limit the scope of his swing.

"It was a private party, dammit!" The boy pushed himself forward, his muscles visibly bunching under the blue T-shirt. There wasn't any excess fat on him; he was athletic and strong and he moved as if he knew it. He still hadn't quite grown into his height, but he wasn't far from it.

Sam shrugged, keeping a wary eye on him. "You got your money back."

"Where's Rimae? I want to see Rimae." He pronounced it Ree-may.

Rimae. That was what Al had said Rita Marie Hoffman was called. This kid was on first-name terms with the owner of the bar? "She's not here yet. I'm sure she'll be happy to listen to you later on."

"Don't you mess with me, Chief," the kid snarled.

He was just a kid, tall and all bones and angles. No match for Sam Beckett, who retained the mental disciplines for a number of martial arts he couldn't remember the names of; no match even for Wickie Gray Wolf Starczynski, who was the same height, not enough older to make a difference, but twenty-five pounds heavier. There was no reason, as far as Sam could see, that the kid should be so sure of himself. The boy was clearly aching for a fight.

Sam wasn't interested in giving it to him. He shrugged

and stepped back, closing the door in the kid's face before the boy could take advantage of the opening. He could keep pounding at it all day, as far as Sam was concerned; all he'd get for it would be bruised knuckles.

He turned back to find himself with an audience: the redoubtable Rimae and two more kids, a girl in her late teens holding the hand of a boy about the same age, or perhaps a little younger. Rimae was standing arms akimbo, with the air of a woman about to deliver serious trouble.

The girl stood at the end of the bar, looking worriedly from Rimae to Sam and back again. She wore pink bell-bottoms that looked a size too small and a loose blouse two sizes too big. She wasn't holding the boy's hand for reassurance but rather to reassure; she whispered something in his ear and edged in front of him protectively.

The boy, by contrast, looked nowhere in particular. Sam's eyes narrowed as he looked at him. There was something—he couldn't quite remember, something nibbling at the back of his mind. It wasn't the way he was dressed; he wore standard-issue jeans and a clean plaid flannel shirt. No, there was something about his appearance. He was thin, not the same kind of coltish adolescent thinness as the argumentative one but as if he'd been starved sometime in an important period of development. His head looked too small for his body.

Probably Davey and Bethica, the adopted son and the niece. If Rita Marie Hoffman was raising two kids, one retarded, as a single woman in the middle 1970s, it said a lot for her courage and determination. He might ask Al just how common that used to be.

Or maybe not. Some genius had made up a rule that he wasn't supposed to know too much about things in the past, for fear that he might change them. He supposed it made sense from one point of view—Heisenberg's—but evidently it had never occurred to the genius in question that the situation might have changed, that the whole point of the exercise *was* to make a change in the past. And it had also never dawned on him that the process of Leaping might make the most inconvenient and erratic holes in the Leaper's memory, so much so that he couldn't always remember from Leap to Leap very much about his own history.

But no, there was a rule, and the overseers of the Project refused to allow Al to provide too much background. He wished he didn't have the unsettling feeling that the genius rulemaker in question was himself. Al had said something to that effect, once or twice.

If he could get to a university with a halfway decent medical library, he could always do a search and try to find out. He'd check and see if Davey's physical characteristics were consistent with something besides simple retardation, too. He was certain they were; they nagged at him the way something blindingly obvious would. It didn't seem likely he'd have the chance to go look it up, though.

In fact, there was some question about whether he was going to get out of this room, judging from the expression on Rimae's face. There was no sign that the attempted seduction of the night before had ever happened.

"Just what was that all about?" she demanded. "And what are you doing over here at this hour, doing Davey's work for him? I've told you a hundred times I don't want you covering up for him. How's he going to learn to do work for himself if you keep covering up for him?"

Sam glanced again at the boy. The kid didn't look the least bit interested in the work or in anything else. It sounded like Wickie covered up for Davey quite a bit. That told him something about Wickie, anyway. He was glad to know the person he'd Leaped into had wider interests than he'd seemed to the night before.

Davey showed a mild flicker of attention at the sound of his name. Bethica soothed him automatically, with the skill of long practice.

"I thought, well, we could get a head start on things," he mumbled. "You know, get everything ready."

"And what's Kevin doing here? I didn't think he'd even be conscious at this hour, much less beating my door down."

Uh-oh. Time to face the music. Sam filed away yet another new name and drew a deep breath. "He's mad because I took the keg back last night," he said. "I gave him his money back."

"You did what?" Rimae's arms dropped. "Say that again?"

"I took the keg up there last night and found out they were all underage kids. So I took it back. I gave him his money back, but he's . . . upset." Sam could have used other words to describe Kevin's state of mind, but the memory of his mother standing over him with a bar of pine tar soap, and the taste of that soap, remained sharp and clear in his memory. One did not use language like that in front of ladies or children.

Absent evidence to the contrary, every female was a lady. Thelma Beckett was quite clear on this point. Young Sam had learned fast. As he'd gotten older, he'd absorbed the lesson into his bones.

"He'd paid for it. He was of age. It's none of our business what happens to it after we sell it. What's wrong with you?"

Sam took a deep breath and closed his eyes. He could always argue about it, but it wouldn't do any good.

"I didn't think it was right," he said.

Rimae stared at him as if she thought her bartender had been suddenly possessed by some benign demon. Her anger was lost in pure bafflement.

"Well, next time do a little less thinking and a little more business, okay?" She shook her head. "I swear I don't know what's gotten into you the last couple of months.

"Where's the keg? Still out in the truck? Go get it and bring it in here. No point in leaving it out there."

Sam heaved a sigh of relief and nodded, headed for the back entrance to the bar. He passed Davey and looked him in the eyes, still searching for some sign of life, of intelligence.

The brown eyes looking back at him were blank, and Sam shivered inside.

He didn't realize he'd been followed until he was outside, trying to pull the door closed. The knob was pulled from his hand as Bethica stepped out.

"Wickie, I wanted to warn you . . ." she began.

But by that time he had seen the new bright red pickup parked next to the Polar Bar's beaten-up old truck, and the two boys struggling with the quarter-keg, trying to get it over the tailgate.

"Hey!" he yelled.

One of the boys looked up, cursed, and ran like a rabbit, leaving Kevin standing in the back end of Wickie's truck looking furious again. Or, perhaps, still.

"What the hell do you want?" Kevin challenged.

Sam stared in disbelief. "Well, for starters, you can put that thing down and get out of that truck."

"This is my property!"

"He's really mad," the girl behind him said, as if Sam needed the clarification.

"Yeah, I can see that," he snapped, a little more harshly than he intended. "Stay out of the way, okay?" He directed his attention back to Kevin, who had set down his end of the keg.

"It isn't your property. You got your money back. Now come on, get out of that truck."

The boy was wavering between jumping out of the truck, which would make it appear that he was obeying Wickie, or remaining where he was, which would rapidly become untenable. Sam held his breath. If Kevin jumped out, he didn't need Ziggy to tell him there would probably be a fight. If Kevin stayed, he had no more idea than the kid did what was going to happen next.

Neither did Kevin. Hesitating a moment, he stared down at the man he knew as Wickie and at Bethica. He started to say something, and Sam stepped out from the building, away from the truck, giving him lots of space.

Inviting him, in fact. And predictably enough, Kevin took the invitation, launching himself over the tailgate and landing with legs bent, scuffing the dirt and gravel. He picked himself up and kept coming.

Once upon a time Sam Beckett had believed that the human animal, like other animals, needed some kind of incentive to attack—some signal from an opponent, some provocation. Somewhere along the line he had lost that belief, like so many other beliefs based in scientific innocence. Human beings didn't operate like animals. Human beings responded like . . . people.

Instead of taking the signal that the older man wasn't offering any threat, Kevin kept coming, pausing only long enough to pick up a stretch of two-by-four and swing it in his direction. Sam ducked, farther away from the building, away from the girl, hoping she had the sense to stay out of the range of the length of wood. He risked a glance back to check, and only the whistling of air warned him to drop flat. Kevin yelled in triumph. Sam rolled, hitting him in the legs, knocking him down, and kept rolling, letting the inertia bring him back to his feet, kicking the board away from Kevin's clawing fingers, dropping to his knees and snatching the boy's left arm up between his shoulder blades, immobilizing him.

"Now suppose we just talk about this," he suggested, breathing hard. "You got your money back, right?" He yanked on the arm, just hard enough to emphasize his words, careful not to do any real damage.

Kevin yelped. Sam yanked again. "Right!"

"And everything's fair and square, right?"

He could see Kevin rolling his eye to try to look at him, and pressed the boy's face into the ground exactly as hard and no harder than needed to keep him from lifting his head. "Everything's fair and square, right?" he repeated. "You got your money back, and we got the keg. Right?"

Kevin squirmed. "Damn you—"

Sam leaned in on him a trifle. "Come on," he said through

his teeth. "Is this worth a damned quarter-keg of beer?"

Kevin snarled something. Sam chose to interpret it as submission, waited one beat, and then let go, getting up and standing well clear. Kevin stirred slowly, getting first to all fours and then sitting back on his haunches, brushing the dirt out of his face with the back of his hand, not meeting Sam's eyes. "You're gonna be sorry for this," he muttered. "You're gonna pay."

"Wouldn't be the first time," Sam said under his breath. He watched as Kevin staggered to his feet, rubbing his shoulder and swinging his arm in a circle, and waited until the boy got into his own truck and pulled out, spraying gravel and broken bits of tar in a long arc across the parking lot. The red truck nearly sideswiped another car as it careened onto the main street.

"He'll come back," the girl behind him said. "He hates you."

"Somehow that doesn't surprise me at all," Sam answered wryly, not turning around.

So he was not in the least prepared when Bethica slipped her arms around him and laid her head against the middle of his back.

"You were really brave," the girl said, giving him a quick, tight hug. He could feel her breath through the cloth between his shoulder blades, and couldn't help squirming at the sensation.

"Ah, no, I wouldn't say so," he stammered, and reached up to remove her hands, stepping out and away and around in one smooth movement.

"But you were!" Her eyes were shining, and she seemed to take no exception to his escape—possibly because he was still holding on to her hands to keep her from grabbing him again. "Wickie, you were great. Kevin's really *mean*. He likes to beat on people."

"I noticed." Where was Al, with the handy handlink to tell him who the devil this Kevin kid was? He had to have something to do with this Leap.

Another thought occurred to him, and he looked at Bethica more carefully. "Does he—'beat on' you?"

Pinkness gathered under her skin, and she looked down at the ground. "No," she said. "Kevin wouldn't ever hit me." She raised her head to look him in the eye. "Besides, I told you, I broke up with him."

She was telling the truth, as far as he could tell. But he'd heard those words before from . . . from Katie, that was it. His little sister, talking about her first husband. *"Chuck wouldn't ever hit me."*

But Chuck had, and Kevin had too, he suspected. He resolved to keep an eye on Bethica—although from the way she behaved, he figured keeping track of Bethica would be the least of his problems. He wondered if Rimae knew her niece had a crush on the bartender, and what effect it would have on Rimae's planned entertainment for Friday nights. Wickie would be lucky to get out of this one alive.

"If he ever tries, you tell me," he said at last. "Promise?"

She ducked her head again and nodded. "I'll tell you," she said gravely.

"I'll take care of Kevin," he said firmly. And hoped that it was true.

CHAPTER

SEVEN

Every other Saturday, Wickie had the night off, and it was an other Saturday tonight. Sam decided to remain in the bar anyway, watching, listening, picking up what information about Snow Owl he could, and giving himself a respite from Rimae, Bethica, and everyone else. He took over the piano bench, idly picking out a tune, nursing a beer along.

The Polar Bar wasn't very well patronized for a Saturday night. Perhaps a dozen couples, half that many unattached men and women, all of whom already knew each other, sat around and talked. They noticed his playing and started to tip him for requests. The Polar Bar wasn't a sophisticated, swinging pickup place. It was a neighborhood bar, where everybody knew his name.

He wondered if Wickie could play. If not, the bartender would have some explaining to do once Sam Leaped out. He'd done something like this before, Sam thought he remembered. He didn't think he'd be involved in any car chases this time, though. At least nobody had waved a gun at him so far. But nobody was asking him to sing, either, and he distinctly remembered that he liked to sing.

He decided not to push it. The tastes of the clientele of the Polar Bar leaned toward country-western, and he did the best he could. Between old Marty Robbins tunes he sneaked in some jazz, and nobody seemed to object.

He would have liked to really cut loose, but he didn't want to call that much attention to himself. Maybe tomorrow, when the bar was closed, he could come back in and practice awhile. For now he ran unfamiliar hands over the yellowed keys and hummed to himself.

He'd spent a couple of hours that way when Rimae Hoffman leaned over him, chuckling deep in her throat. Wreaths of cigarette smoke surrounded her head, and Sam had to force himself not to make a face at the mixed smells of lilac perfume and tobacco.

"You keep surprising me," she said, making no particular effort to keep her voice down. "You're a man of hidden talents."

"More than you could ever guess," Sam responded, feeling a sudden need to watch where he put his hands.

"Oh, I'm finding out." She expelled streams of smoke from her mouth and nostrils, looked around for an ashtray, and discovered Sam had moved it several tables farther away. She brought it back with her, mashing the cigarette down. "Bethica says you got into a fight with Kevin Hodge about that keg this morning. I keep telling you, baby, don't bruise the paying customers."

Sam shook his head, not sure what to say.

Someone else came by, stuck a dollar into a glass on top of the piano, and requested "Please Believe Me." He sighed and did the best he could from the memory of the melody and unskilled hands, only having to start over twice. Rimae waited until he was finished, leaning on the piano and smiling at him, her hand curled around a glass. She wore bright red fingernail polish on short, workmanlike nails. Worn down instead of piled up, and styled in a casual flip, her teased hair was medium length. Her skin was dark, almost leathery with repeated tanning, her face lined by character and weathering.

She must have dyed her hair since last night, Sam thought. No gray roots showed now. Her makeup was less vivid than it had been the night before, too. She had character in her face, ironic humor in her bright blue eyes—not like Bethica's, Bethica's eyes were the soft blue of cornflowers while Rimae's were crystalline, glittering, outlined in kohl and spiky lashes.

And she was watching him as if she knew something about him and it amused her. At least she wasn't furious at him any more. The look in her eyes wasn't angry, that was for sure. Speculative, perhaps. Possessive.

This was the time, he thought, that Al should pop in, making some snide comment about Rimae still having the hots for him. And she did, he could tell, even without the incident of the previous night. It was that look.

But Al never showed. He kept playing, not meeting Rimae's eyes, until she finally laughed her throaty laugh again and took herself and her cigarettes over behind the bar to talk to the woman handling the Saturday-night shift. He sneaked a glance after her as she swayed away. It was a shame Al was missing this; black satin toreador pants, a concho belt with sandcast silver links three inches square, a white blouse with layers of frothy lace at collar and cuffs. It might have looked cliché, but it wasn't. Conversation swirled around her and followed her as she greeted the patrons that she passed.

His hands rippled out a few bars from "The Girl From Ipanema" all on their own, and he shook his head in disgust and got up. He debated a moment about the tips in the glass, decided Wickie could probably use the money, took it and stuffed it into a pocket of his jeans. He could always count it later and leave Wickie a note of the total for tax purposes.

Smiling, he finished his beer in one long swallow and waved away the two or three voices raised in protest as he slipped out the front door of the bar, closing off the noise of it with the closing of the door. He paused to take a deep breath of the chilly night air, clearing the smell of tobacco smoke from his lungs, and looked around at the litter of cars nuzzled up to the building. Family cars, most of them. The summer economy of Snow Owl didn't lend itself to Jaguars and Mercedes.

He could smell steaks grilling somewhere in someone's backyard barbecue, tangy in the mountain air. He followed the smell away from the noise and lights and cars until he found himself standing in the trees, pine needles crunching under the soles of his shoes. The smell faded and was replaced by the perfume of pine trees as the breeze changed direction, and he stood still, eyes closed, listening to the night.

The pine needles, whispering in the breeze. Some small creature rustling through the twigs. Behind him, the sounds of people laughing together. There, off to the right, a dog barking.

He turned thirty degrees, tilted his head to catch other sounds: the almost inaudible thrumming of wind in an owl's wings, the chirping of a cicada. A car door slamming far away. A rustling, gurgling sound of a mountain stream, only a few feet away.

How often did he get a chance to just stand alone in the darkness, not thinking about anything, just listening? How often did he have the chance to breathe deep of clean air, feel the movement of air on his face and not be afraid?

Sometimes it *was* good for a man to be alone.

For a little while, anyway. Shaking off the mood, he opened his eyes again and oriented himself on the neon lights of the Polar Bar, sighed and stuck his hands in his pockets and began to trudge back.

He was beginning to wonder about Al. He couldn't remember—well, he *couldn't*, eidetic memory notwithstanding, and a lot of good it did him with holes punched into it—the last time Al had let more than twenty-four hours go by before renewing contact with him. Sometimes it took a while for Ziggy to find him, but once the computer locked on, Al was always prompt to appear. And once he made first contact, he maintained it.

Not this time, though. Well, granted that he'd chased the

Observer off, but that was an old story by this time, and it shouldn't have kept Al away this long.

He rounded the back of Wickie's cabin, wondering, and a pile of bricks fell on him.

Well, it *felt* like a pile of bricks, anyway. It was Davey, jumping from the roof in the darkness, a sheet tied around his neck to make a great, flapping, lightweight cloak. He grunted as he hit Sam, flailing around and getting more and more tangled up in the sheet. Sam picked himself up, brushed himself off, and looked from the boy still sprawled in the dirt to the low roof of the cabin and back again.

"I did that once," he admitted to no one in particular.

Davey stopped thrashing long enough to give him a sidelong glance and went back to fighting the sheet.

"Hey, wait a minute," Sam said, becoming alarmed as the sheet, as if with a mind of its own, twisted around the boy's neck. "Hold on. Calm down."

He found himself using the same tone he'd use to a frightened animal, even, soothing, steady. Davey responded in much the same way. His face was curiously blank through it all, showing no anger or fear; he held still while Sam worked the knot loose and unwrapped the material, then he got up and grabbed the sheet away.

"Hey, wait a minute!" Sam repeated. "Where do you think you're going with that?"

"Gonna fly," Davey said. He stepped away.

"Not with that, you're not. It doesn't work. Didn't you just figure that out?"

"Gonna fly." Now the boy was shaking the sheet out, taking two of the corners to tie around his neck once more. Sam had a sudden chilling vision of it getting caught on something, of Davey hanging—

"No," he said. "Give it to me, Davey."

"Gonna fly." Davey swung the sheet around behind himself.

"*No,*" Sam said again. He caught at the boy's hands. "No, Davey."

"Fly."

"No. This won't help you fly." When Sam was three, he tested a Superman hypothesis. He wondered what cartoons Davey watched that still featured superheroes who wore capes and flew, for truth, justice, and putting things right that once went wrong.

Davey was still looking at him blankly. He wasn't getting through. Sam took a deep breath and a good hold on the sheet and tried to take it away.

Davey was small, and wiry, and tough, and not about to give up his dream. He fought back, or rather pulled away, and Sam found himself engaged in a tug-of-war across the half-empty rear parking lot of the bar. Against Davey's wiriness he pitted Wickie's size and weight. In short order he was nose to nose with Davey, who would not surrender his last few inches of cotton sheet. Sam had to pry his fingers loose, one by one, and then hope the kid wouldn't come around behind him to pick up the excess and start the whole thing over again.

But Davey didn't. He looked down at his hands once the sheet had been prized loose, and then at the swath of cotton material, and turned and shambled away without speaking, leaving Sam with his hands full of bedsheet, feeling silly and sad and a lot like a bully. All the kid wanted to do was fly, after all. It wasn't so very much.

He wadded up the sheet—he wasn't sure it could be salvaged after being dragged around and ground into the asphalt and gravel, but he had to try—and went back to Wickie's cabin, wishing there was some way to get through to the boy. When he paused for a last look over his shoulder, Davey had disappeared around the end of the building. Sam shook his head. His cabin door was unlocked. He flicked on the light and paused.

He stood in the doorway and looked around. He might not be able to remember locking the door, but he knew he hadn't left the cabin in this condition.

The few books Wickie had were in tatters, the leaves

scattered as if a tornado had hit the room. White powder, a mixture of flour and sugar, drifted over everything. Everything breakable was broken; shards of glass glittered on the floor. Unidentifiable, stinking liquids stained the walls, the furniture, pooled on flat surfaces. Obscene words were scrawled on the pictures. A pile of excrement sat in the middle of the rug, still steaming.

He didn't even want to think about what the kitchen must look like.

"Oh, no," said a small voice from behind him. "Oh, this is awful."

He didn't have to glance around to know it was Bethica. "I'd have to agree with you there," he said. "I hope there's cleaning supplies around here somewhere. Still in their containers, I mean."

"Ooo, is that—that's dis*gust*ing." Bethica had just gotten a good look at the final insult on the rug. "Oh, wow." She slipped around him and tiptoed around the worst damage, making faces as she went. "Gross." She paused to pick up what remained of the algebra book and some papers, examined them, and sighed. "Even the problems we were doing. That dork." Stepping into the kitchen, she added, "Oh, this is *really* bad."

"That's what I was afraid of," Sam muttered. He made as if to drop the sheet and decided not to; it was probably the cleanest fabric in the place. He wondered if Wickie owned a washer and dryer, and doubted it.

Well, there had to be a laundromat somewhere in town. At least he didn't have to worry about how he was going to spend the rest of the night.

Bethica returned to the living room with a broom and a black metal dustpan. "I could get started in here," she said. "But we're going to need a lot of stuff. Trash bags and stuff."

He liked her immediate, pragmatic approach. Bethica might have a crush on him—on Wickie, he corrected himself—but she was also a thoroughly practical kid.

73

"I don't suppose there's an all-night grocery store around here?" Sam asked without thinking. He found himself wondering why she was there.

Bethica looked at him oddly. "The ShopRite closes at ten."

Of course. He should have known that.

He'd gotten odder looks than hers. Glancing at his watch, he saw that it was nine-fifteen. It surprised him; he'd thought it was later than that. "I guess I'd better go, then." It was a good thing Snow Owl wasn't a very big place; it should be fairly easy to find the store. He looked up at Bethica. "I don't think you'd better stay here, though. Whoever did this could come back."

" 'Whoever did this'?" she repeated, reprising the odd look. "Wickie, we both *know* who did this. He's been mad at you ever since—ever since I gave you that book. And when you took back the keg in front of everybody, that just made it worse."

Sam realized abruptly that Bethica had been one of the kids up at the party when he'd Leaped in. "You were there, too? I thought you were smarter than that."

She gave him the long-suffering look teenagers always gave adults who said stupid things, and changed the subject. "I'll get started," she said. "He isn't going to come back."

Sam contemplated calling the cops, saw the dangling wires where the telephone had been torn out of the wall, and decided against it. It would be entirely too easy to turn Kevin over to the cops, but he could figure out for himself what the odds were that the boy would be out on bail in no time flat, and not feeling any more charitable toward either Wickie *or* Bethica.

He wished Al would show up and give him some idea how he was supposed to handle this.

"It isn't safe," he protested halfheartedly.

"The store's going to close," she pointed out, and went into the kitchen and proceeded to make sweeping-up noises.

She was right. Sighing, he hugged the sheet to himself and went out to the truck.

CHAPTER
EIGHT

Al Calavicci had spared a thought to his best friend at least three times that day. Each time, he asked Ziggy how Sam was doing. Each time, upon being informed that the computer was unable as yet to define a probability locus and that Sam was in no apparent danger, he returned to exploring the wonders of amicable married life.

He avoided thinking about the past; it was too confusing, for one thing, and for another, he wasn't quite sure which memories went with which past. He couldn't put his finger on exactly where the timelines diverged.

But he knew he liked Janna more and more every minute. She was sharp and funny and gave as good as she got. And she could scramble eggs like nobody's business.

Even when breakfast was oatmeal.

Ziggy couldn't provide an answer, either, on what the odds were that this particular timeline would remain stable. The next time Al entered the Imaging Chamber, this entire "moment" might vanish as if it had never been.

Under the circumstances, he felt justified in delaying, just a little bit, going back to check on Sam. Especially since Sam wasn't in any danger, or anything.

Besides, it was Saturday at the Project too, and he could take the day off. He and Janna could run up to Albuquerque and do some shopping. Maybe even catch dinner and a concert in Santa Fe—the King-Aire could land on the Santa Fe airstrip. It wasn't as if he were going off to Washington. And he hadn't had time off in a long time.

Sam found the ShopRite twenty minutes before it closed, swept in, and bought everything he could think of. He was the last customer. "You planning on starting your own business, Wickie?" the cashier asked him, ringing up the last pack of sponges and figuring the rental charge for the rug shampooer.

So much for pretending he was new in town and asking where the nearest all-night laundromat was.

"Just decided to do some cleaning up," he mumbled, watching the total grow. It was a good thing he did collect those tips, as it turned out; he just barely had enough. The cashier gave him a pretty smile with his change. It was a nice moment. The whole evening had been pretty nice, in fact, right up until he got home.

Arms full of paper bags, he trudged back to the truck and set them in the back. There were only four other vehicles in the parking lot.

From one of them, a red pickup, came the sounds of adolescent male laughter.

He drew a deep breath, got in the truck and drove back to the cabin.

Bethica was in the bathroom, throwing up. Looking around, he couldn't blame her. He put the bags down and began putting chairs right side up. It was going to be a very, very long night.

Ten minutes later, Bethica was still in the bathroom throwing up, the most noxious part of the cleanup job was out of the way, and Sam wanted to wash his hands. He tapped on the door.

"Bethica? You okay in there?" The sound of retching made him gag in sympathy.

"Yeah," she said in a faint and completely unconvincing voice. The toilet flushed. The door opened three inches, and

76

she peered up at him. She didn't look well. "I tried to clean the rug and . . . I think I'm going to be sick again."

It was essential to save her dignity. It was even more essential to let her get back to the toilet. "Don't let me stop you," he said hastily.

Bethica staggered back, swinging the door open, and lunged for the bowl again. Sam followed her, keeping an eye on her as he scrubbed at his hands. From the looks of it, she'd managed to get the bathroom sparkling before succumbing to nausea; he was pretty sure he'd had to shave around water streaks on the mirror that morning. The pink razor, soap, and loofah were all gone, he noticed.

Finally his hands were raw from scrubbing. Bethica was still clinging to the bowl.

"Hey, are you sure you're okay?" He got down on one knee beside her and lifted her head, cautiously. She was pale and red eyed and her face was streaked with tears, and she looked nothing like the practical woman who had started cleaning up while he went shopping. He looked around, scrabbled one handed in a drawer underneath the sink, and found a clean washcloth, soaking it in cold water.

"Hey there." He washed her face clean with the impersonal efficiency and expertise of a good nurse, and she burst into tears again.

If Al was going to show up, he thought, it would be right now, to see him sitting on the bathroom floor with a teenage girl in his arms, crying her heart out. He'd either make some snide crack or overflow with sympathy. Maybe both. Simultaneously. Meanwhile, the best he could do was try to soothe the girl and figure out how to get them out of the bathroom.

"Sorry," she said at last, straightening up and making a valiant effort to pretend she'd never cried at all. "I don't know why it got to me like that. I used to have to clean up after Davey all the time. I guess it's just the *idea* anybody would do such a thing." She sniffled, and despite herself a line of tears escaped and threaded down her cheek. "I'm really sorry he did this, Wickie. Really. He has no *right* to treat you this way."

She shook her head back and forth, blonde hair flying. She didn't hold up well, he decided. Some women shed beautiful tears, elegant, long suffering, perfect for a follow spot in the movies. Bethica snuffled. Sam gave up.

"It's disgusting," he agreed, "but it's not your fault. Are you sure you're okay?" He scrubbed fresh tear tracks away, and she sat there and let him, like a little girl, not a teenager only a few years younger than he—Wickie—was. He took the opportunity to check her face for bruises—he still didn't believe her claim that Kevin didn't hit her—but found none.

"I don't know what's wrong with me," she said, beginning to look around. He moved back so she could stand. "It's such a mess. It just hit me so hard—"

"That can happen when you're pregnant," Sam said without thinking. "It's normal. Your hormones are out of whack."

Bethica's head snapped around so fast he had an instant of worry for her neck. "*What* did you say?"

He opened his mouth to repeat himself and then paused, reviewing unconscious cues. "How long has it been since you had your period?"

The look on her face reminded him that Wickie Starczynski was no doctor, and the question was probably far more intimate than Wickie's relationship with his boss's niece warranted. Chagrined, he tried to apologize. "I mean, you *are* pregnant, aren't you?"

She shook her head and blew her nose, took a deep breath, and got up without looking at him. "That's . . . that's none of your business."

She didn't know, he realized abruptly. She had no idea she was pregnant. She probably thought she was just late, or skipped a period. His eyes narrowed again: maybe two periods. Those jeans *were* getting tight.

But there was nothing in the information he had so far that indicated Bethica's pregnancy had anything to do with anything. He sighed. "You're right, it isn't. Look, Bethica, I really appreciate your help here, but I think you'd better get home—"

It was the wrong thing to say. He followed her back into the kitchen to dig through the grocery sacks for the Kleenex, borrowing one to blow his nose while he was at it—something in the air was making his nose run and his eyes water and itch.

In the act of turning to throw the tissue away he paused. An odd, scraping sound was coming from the living room; Bethica, who was standing at the sink wringing out a sponge, didn't appear to hear it.

If Kevin *had* come back—

He moved as silently as possible to the door and stuck his head around the frame.

At first the room appeared empty. He stepped into the doorway.

Scrape. Scrape. Scrape.

Scrape.

The sound drew his gaze downward, to a small, chubby grey tabby kitten who seemed to feel that the rug shampooer hadn't done an adequate job. She sniffed again at the rug, curled her lip.

Scrape. Scrape.

"Achoo!"

Sam wasn't sure who was more startled by his sneeze, but judging by the reaction, the kitten won by a long margin; she levitated straight up, came down on the arm of the sofa, bounced to the back of the sofa, threw one terrified yellow glance at Sam, the cat-devouring monster looming in the doorway, and jumped down and dived underneath, out of sight.

"Achoo!"

On top of everything else, it appeared that Wickie was allergic to cats.

Sam knew of some cat lovers who kept the animals in the face of the most debilitating allergies, but there had

79

been no sign of kitty litter, cat food, or water dishes in the cabin. The kitten was, therefore, not Wickie's. He hadn't reacted to it before Bethica arrived. Deductive logic led inevitably to the conclusion: The kitten arrived with, and must therefore belong to, Bethica. Sam hoped the kid could get the little beast out and take it with her when she left. He didn't look forward to sneezing all night.

He made a mental note to tell her not to feed her pet so much. The kitten had the dimensions of a furry butterball. He wiped at his streaming eyes again.

Which reminded him that he'd been in the middle of an errand of mercy when he'd been so rudely interrupted.

Bethica had finished with the sponge and was emptying out a bucket. She took the proffered tissue gratefully. "I knew," she said abruptly. "I've been making plans. I'll deal with it, okay?"

"Okay," Sam said helplessly.

Her eyes fell. "You must think I'm pretty dumb, don't you?"

"Not necessarily." As a matter of fact he wasn't sure what he *did* think, except that it was getting rather late for a Saturday evening, and if Rimae showed up, there might well be consequences of a nature better dealt with by, say, Al, who at least had more practice. "I'm not making any judgments. You've got to tell Rimae, though."

She shot him an incredulous look. "She'll kill me."

"I don't think so. She'll be pretty mad, though. But you can't put it off much longer."

Bethica's lips firmed. "That's my business, too."

Sam sighed and gave up. "Okay, fine. If that's the way you want to play it. Look, I really appreciate the help, but I think you'd better go home now. Let me walk you over, and I'll finish cleaning up."

"I don't need to be walked home." She was getting angry again. Well, anger was a valid coping mechanism too.

"If you need somebody to talk to—" he offered, unable to stop himself. Her glare did it for him. "Oh, your cat is in the living room," he said hastily, changing the subject. "I think you'd better take her with you."

Once again, he'd said the wrong thing. "I don't have a cat. But I can take a hint." Pushing past him, she dropped the used Kleenex into the wastebasket and marched through the cabin and out the door.

"Some Leaps you just can't win," Sam muttered. He became aware of yellow eyes, huge in the small triangular face, outlined by dark lids and white stripes, observing him steadily from under the sofa. The watcher had two dark vertical strips like exclamation points over her nose. He could probably hold her in one hand, he thought, watching her in return. "Boo!"

The kitten hastily withdrew.

He followed Bethica at a distance to the house at the end of the block, making sure she got home all right. She paused briefly in the porchlight, looking back at him, and he raised one hand, tentatively. She raised one in return. With that much comfort, he went back to the cabin to finish the cleanup.

The next several hours were punctuated with sneezes. He needed more tissue; two boxes weren't enough. He had to wash down the walls, sweep up more debris, and put bag after overstuffed bag of garbage out the front door. The kitten supervised. After the first hour she decided he was mostly harmless, and crept out from under the sofa to go back into her "you missed a spot" routine again. When Sam didn't respond—other than to sneeze—the kitten mewed half a mew at him.

"What are you, a cat or a mouse?"

The kitten made an ek-ek sound, and then began to purr, a surprisingly deep rumble for such a small body, and stropped herself against his ankles.

"Ah, shaddup, ach-ch-ch—"

Scrape. Scrape. Scrape.

"—oo. You wouldn't know where Al is, would you?"

The cat didn't know either.

It was four-thirty in the morning before Sam finally straightened up, looked around, and decided it would have to do. The kitten had long since given up on him and curled up in the corner of the sofa, which it clearly regarded as its own personal property. Judging by the amount of grey hair already liberally scattered over the rough plaid surface, Sam wasn't inclined to argue. He'd be happy to let the cat have the sofa, at least for the remainder of the night, as long as he could have the rest of the house. Specifically the bed.

He'd forgotten about house cats and beds, especially when the door had been torn off its hinges and there wasn't any way to keep them out of the bedroom. Some five minutes after his head hit the pillow, little cat feet began marching up his leg to his hip, kneaded, and settled. He moaned and went back to sleep, acknowledging defeat.

SUNDAY

June 8, 1975

But he who loveliness within
Hath found, all outward loathes,
For he who color loves, and skin,
Loves but their oldest clothes.
      —**John Donne**, *The Undertaking*, st. 4

CHAPTER NINE

The next morning he woke to the sound of prerecorded church bells. The cat was gone, much to his relief. Probably off somewhere looking for food. At least the bags of trash on the porch were intact.

He wondered if he should tell Rimae about the cabin getting trashed before she noticed the broken windows. Based on the way she'd reacted about the truck, she probably wasn't going to be too happy about it. It was a shame, too, considering she seemed to have forgiven him about the keg.

He wondered if he could find a glazier open on a Sunday. Probably not; he'd have to try to get it done tomorrow morning. Monday.

Monday was the day of the party. The day of the wreck. Which might or might not be going to happen, and Al hadn't come back to let him know. Not since Friday night.

Bethica was supposed to be involved in that wreck, he remembered. So this Leap did involve her. He wondered if it involved her baby, too. He wished Al would show up so they could figure things out. Did Bethica tell Rimae about the baby? Did she lose it, give it up, abort it?

He found himself considering the possibilities with an objectivity that he would once have said he didn't possess. Too much experience with Leaping had changed him; it wasn't like him to be so detached from the people around him. A lot of things were unlike him, Sam decided. He'd been wondering for a while, in fact, just what "like him" was supposed to mean anyway. He taped paper over the broken windows and went back over to the bar.

Davey was already there, sweeping the floor. Rimae was behind the bar, setting clean glasses back in place. The boy spared him not so much as a glance. Rimae looked up indifferently. "Oh, there you are."

"Here I am," Sam agreed, and wondered if he too had some assigned task.

"You're spending a lot of your free time around here lately," Rimae said. She was checking stock now, counting bottles and making notes on a clipboard. "What's the matter, aren't there any more fish in the creek out there?"

No assigned task. Well. He considered telling her about the vandalism, decided not to. Maybe he could get the windows fixed before she found out. The rest of the place was in pretty good shape—better than when he'd Leaped in.

He sat down again on the piano bench. The presence of Rimae and her son put a hole in his plans for the piano; he had a feeling the classics would be out of character. Wickie wasn't a Rimsky-Korsakov kind of guy.

But he was unable to keep his hands off the keys. Rimae looked up as the first notes began to ripple through the air, snorted and went back to what she was doing.

Davey, on the other hand, stopped sweeping to watch him. Sam registered the change in activity level, looked up and smiled at him.

The broom clattered to the floor, and Davey came over to stand beside him.

"He's always liked music," Rimae called out. Sam gave out with a jaunty jazz riff.

Davey grinned, a stiff and awkward smile, reached out and began pounding on the keys in the upper register, a pounding completely out of sync with Sam's playing, dissonant, unrhythmic, harsh.

Sam stopped at once. "Would you like to play?"

Davey nodded jerkily and continued pounding. Sam caught at his hands. "Hey, hold on. Let me show you." He moved over to make room on the bench for the boy.

As soon as he took his hands away, Davey resumed pounding at the keys.

"No," Sam said. "Sit down." This time he held on to the boy's hands until Davey was seated beside him.

"Now look." He let go to demonstrate the first three notes of "Chopsticks." Davey instantly pounded on the keys.

Rimae chuckled. "Now you've got him going," she said, polishing the top of the bar. "He won't quit."

Sam had the feeling she might be right, but he wasn't ready to give up yet. "That's quite a tune you're playing, Davey," he said soothingly. "That's a good tune. Would you like to learn another good tune? Then you'll have two of them." *And the piano might survive a little longer*, he added to himself.

He placed Davey's hands—small, bony hands—on the proper keys and pressed down. *Oh, Nicole, if you could only see me now*, he thought wryly. *I'll bet you never had a student like this one.* Nicole had been his piano teacher when he was younger than Davey was now. And in about—Sam calculated absently—four years from now, she'd be hired as an understudy for an out-of-town production of *Man of La Mancha*, and she'd meet a man she used to know and love. Only it would be Sam Beckett.

It was still the future for her. It was part of the past for Sam, one of innumerable loops of the past. He still thought about her. She had been, would be, a wonderful teacher, in more ways than one. " 'Sancho, my armor!' " he whispered to himself, smiling wistfully. The boy sitting beside him didn't notice.

Davey let Sam move his hands, unresisting, over the keys. He didn't cooperate, either. Sam couldn't even tell if the boy understood that the music was being played as a result of his pressing the keys. He stared at the yellowed ivory uncomprehendingly.

Sam moved his hands through the pattern once, twice, three times. "There. See? Now you try it."

Davey went back to indiscriminate pounding.

Rimae laughed. "Now you know why I keep that old piano closed up," she said. "But you play pretty good."

"Ever tried teaching him?" Sam asked, trying to catch hold of Davey's hands again. He finally succeeded. Holding them with one of his own, he pulled the cover closed.

Davey recognized at once that he could no longer reach the black and white keys. He touched the wood of the cover, an oddly light touch, sighed, and then got up, went back to pick up his broom, and resumed sweeping, all without saying a word.

"He's always been that way," Rimae said, shrugging. "Slow." There was regret in her voice, but no self-pity, and no pity for Davey, either. He simply *was,* and she obviously refused to think of it in terms of something "wrong" with the boy. He was slow, that was all. He was hers. Sam remembered seeing Bethica, the morning before, protectively holding Davey's hand, and decided Rimae's acceptance wasn't the worst thing in the world to pass on to her niece.

Davey dropped the broom on the floor and ran out the door. Rimae looked at Sam and shrugged.

Retarded. Handicapped. Intellectually challenged. There were half a dozen ways of saying it; they all came to the same thing, in greater or lesser degrees of tact and political correctness. But the physical markers indicated there was something more at work, too. He knew what it was, he just couldn't . . . quite . . . put a name to it yet. Ziggy could tell him what it was, no doubt.

But where the hell was Al?

"I'm going to be in my office, working on the books this afternoon," Rimae said at last. "Bethie'll look after Davey, if you want to stop on by for your check."

He looked up to see her smiling at him, wondering if there was a double meaning in her words. And even if there was, there wasn't anything he could do about it. For the time being, he was stuck here.

Al was engaged in coating the inside of a sopaipilla with honey, watching as Janna did the same thing. A trickle of golden fluid dribbled out of a hole in the pillow-shaped bread and dripped along her little finger, and she sucked at it. He smiled to himself.

"Do I have to ask what you're thinking?" she scolded him, smiling back. "You've got that look on your face again."

"I'm just wondering what this expedition's going to cost," he improvised. "And we haven't even gone to any of the galleries on Water Street yet." He looked at the stack of packages at her feet. "And a good thing, too."

"It was your idea," she pointed out.

They were having Sunday brunch in the La Fonda Hotel in Santa Fe, just off the Plaza. The ceiling arched three stories over their heads. The room was decorated in soft pinks and blues, the colors of adobe and turquoise, and the tables were rough-dressed wood covered with woven cotton mats. Trees grew up in the middle of the room, sheltering them from the gaze of the inquisitive. The voices of other diners, the sound of cutlery and ceramic dinnerware, were lost in the huge room.

"It's been a long time since we've been able to do something like this," Janna observed. "I can't even remember the last time."

"Neither can I," Al said with absolute truth. They'd arrived Saturday afternoon, walked through the Plaza hand in hand, and decided to stay over after the concert, something with banjos that hadn't interfered with his enjoyment of her company. This morning they'd gotten up early—she was a morning person—and roamed around the shops and museums. "It's like a whole new life."

Janna glanced up at him through long lashes, puzzled. He shook his head and dug into the chicken enchiladas.

"Don't you feel the least bit guilty?" she asked. "I mean, I do. You don't often leave Sam hanging this way. Two whole days."

"I didn't leave him hanging." Al's voice was sharper than he meant it to be. "He's okay. Ziggy would tell me if there were any problems."

Ziggy was supposed to tell him what Sam was supposed to do on this Leap, too, but the computer hadn't said anything yet. The original scenario had shivered and disappeared almost as soon as Sam got there, and Ziggy couldn't nail down what else was supposed to happen. Al was beginning to feel a little uneasy about that, and he resented the feeling. Why couldn't he just enjoy himself for once?

The woman sitting across from him—his *wife*; it was beginning to sink in—raised one hand. "Hold on, Admiral. Pull back the fighter squadrons. You're not under attack. At least," she added thoughtfully, "I don't think you are. Maybe you are. Or maybe I'm just feeling guilty because we spent so much money."

"That would be a switch."

Janna glared. She was beautiful when she glared.

"On the other hand," he went on, "the dress looks good, the jewelry is terrific, the painting . . . well, the painting sucks pond water, but *you* like it, so it works for me."

"You have no appreciation for great art."

"I appreciate great art just fine. Cows wearing overalls don't cut it." He cut another mouthful of enchilada. "Naked ladies, on the other hand—"

"One naked lady at a time," Janna said, nipping at a sopaipilla corner.

He grinned.

She grinned back, nipped at the golden bread again, her white teeth clicking as they met.

"I understand there's an art exhibit going on upstairs this afternoon," she added, dribbling honey quite deliberately down the palm of her hand and licking at it.

Al raised both eyebrows and pushed his plate away. "Upstairs?"

The only thing upstairs that he could think of at the moment was their hotel room. He hadn't checked out; he'd assumed she was going to take care of that.

"It's a *private* exhibit," she added.

"With naked ladies?" he said, experiencing some difficulty with his voice. Maybe her idea of taking care was more in line with his own than he'd thought.

"Only one," she whispered, taking several bills from her purse and placing them on the table.

"One is fine. If it's the right one." He looked at the dripping sopaipilla. "Hey, save some of that for me!"

She chuckled, got to her feet and held out her unsticky hand to him.

I'll catch up with you later, Sam, was Al's last rational thought. *I will. Really.*

He snagged the container of honey from the table as they left.

Bethica walked along the stream behind the line of cabins, kicking at a rock, keeping half an eye on Davey to make sure he didn't fall into the little stream. Wickie was in the bar, talking to Rimae. Telling her about how his place got trashed, probably. Telling her about the baby?

No. He'd said he wouldn't tell, and Wickie didn't lie. That left everything up to her, and she didn't want to believe it. Didn't want to think about it. But it was true; he was right.

She'd been awake all last night, staring up at the ceiling, touching her belly. There was a baby in there. Her baby.

Kevin's baby.

It was hard to connect that thought to the party six weeks ago up the mountain, celebrating Kevin's admission to USC. It was some party. Lots of food, lots of booze, the night

91

cold enough to make cuddling together under the blankets logical, sensible, practical.

She glanced up through the trees to the cabin on the far end. Wickie probably hadn't seen the spray paint on the back door yet.

That Kevin, he could be really disgusting sometimes. She could remember him doing things clear back to the first grade, breaking people's windows, vandalizing schoolrooms. He'd never got caught. Nobody turned in Kevin. They thought it was funny. Sometimes they helped.

Davey had found a piece of wood and was drawing channels for the mountain water, prying rocks out of the way. Where did he think the water would go, she wondered. No matter how hard he tried, it would eventually return to its channel again.

The day after that celebration up on the mountain, Kevin had invited Davey up to his house. Bethica had found him with a bunch of the boys, spinning a blindfolded Davey around and around, edging him toward the Hodges' swimming pool. Kevin knew Davey couldn't swim. He thought it was funny. She had looked into Kevin's eyes over the head of her foster brother and seen only anger at having his game frustrated.

She and Kevin had broken up that day. It was the hardest thing she'd ever done. She'd taken Davey to Wickie, who would never allow anything to harm him, and told Wickie never to allow Kevin anywhere near Davey again. She didn't have to explain why. She'd been so *angry* with Kevin—She could still remember the look in Wickie's dark eyes—relief, perhaps, that she'd finally grown up.

Now she was older than she'd ever intended to be. Her hand rested on her belt buckle, and she wondered what she was supposed to do. She might tell Wickie she had things under control, but really, Rimae was going to be so *mad* at her—

That stuff in Wickie's living room, that was the worst. How could Kevin do something like that? She could feel

92

herself gagging again at the memory, and hastily placed a hand over her mouth.

The worst part was, she was pretty sure he wasn't finished, either. He was angry with her for breaking up with him, and he blamed Wickie. That business about the keg just made it that much worse. Wickie wasn't afraid of Kevin, but he didn't really know how bad he could be. He never gave up, never ever. And he was really angry about that keg.

Wickie acted like he didn't care at all what Kevin did.

He was different. She couldn't put her finger on it, but he was definitely different. When he first came to Snow Owl, he'd looked at her with those dark, dark Indian eyes—they used to be blank, indifferent. As if he didn't know who she was and didn't care. Not just her, either; he looked at everybody that way.

Everybody except Davey. Wickie had always been really good with Davey. And ever since that day, he'd looked at her like a person, a real person. She'd gotten to know him better in the last few weeks than she ever thought she would. All the kids made fun of him, called him a dumb, drunk Indian who worked at the bar for free booze. He wasn't that way, she knew for sure. He was smart and he was kind, even if he never talked about the future and school the way everybody else she knew did. Well, he wasn't one of them, after all.

She looked around. Davey was sitting cross-legged in the mud, drawing lines with his stick. A blue jay was screaming at him. He didn't notice. She got up and stretched and walked over to watch. Davey never looked up.

She couldn't figure out Wickie and Rimae. Wickie didn't care about Rimae, not really. He'd never looked at Rimae the way he ought to. He never talked about her. She asked him about her once and he just looked at her, his eyes back to being flat and cold all of a sudden.

She could feel herself blushing.

And then she remembered how it felt to be folded up in Wickie's arms, and she wondered if that was the way

93

Rimae felt about him, and she blushed even worse, and kicked really hard at a rock and missed, and had to grab at a tree trunk to keep from falling in the stupid creek.

A curl of birch bark dug into her fingers. Catching her balance, she looked to see if her hand was covered with blood. There wasn't any, and she experienced a vague regret. If Wickie held her head while she threw up, he'd pay attention to a bloody hand, wouldn't he?

But there wasn't even a bruise, and she sighed.

She ought to go home. Fix lunch for Davey.

There was supposed to be a party tomorrow night up at the clearing. She wondered if Kevin would get his keg this time. Probably; Rimae had been selling to him as soon as he turned nineteen last February. She wondered if Rimae would have changed her mind if she knew what Kevin and Bethica had done up on the mountainside six weeks ago. Would Rimae care? Would she blame Kevin, or her, or the beer?

Yes, she acknowledged. She'd be mad about it, but she would care.

She had to tell Kevin about the baby. He was the father, after all. He deserved to know.

And maybe that would take his mind off Wickie.

She could tell Kevin, and then tell Rimae, and then what? Get an abortion?

She shivered and pressed on her belt buckle again. Maybe Wickie was wrong?

But Wickie wasn't wrong. Her breasts were getting larger, more sensitive; she was getting sick in the mornings; her period hadn't come; her moods were swinging wildly all over the place.

She didn't *want* to be pregnant. She wanted to be a kid for a while longer, go to parties like the one tomorrow night up on the mountainside, pretend nothing had happened.

She'd go. Just because Kevin was a jerk wasn't any reason to miss a party. All her other friends would be there.

94

She wondered if Wickie liked to party. Besides with Rimae, that is. The image of the two of them made her giggle, embarrassed. Rimae was *old*. Nice enough, maybe; she liked living in the house down the road from the Polar Bar, and Rimae was cool, but she sure was funny about Wickie.

Maybe she could talk Kevin into leaving Wickie alone. She could tell him Wickie knew better than to mess with him now.

She scrunched up her face and peered up through the leaves, mature green now, not pale and new any more.

Yeah. She'd talk to Kevin. He'd listen to her. He owed her that much. He was a jerk, but he *owed* her now.

Davey was standing now, looking around, the stick hanging forgotten from his hand.

It was time to get home. It was long past lunchtime, and Davey was getting hungry.

The bar was empty, and Sam finally had the chance to play whatever he wanted to play without interruption, without an audience, without a damned Observer who was taking his own sweet time about showing up. His hands crashed down on the keys with as much force as Davey had used, and he closed his eyes and breathed deep, as deeply as he could, clear down to the diaphragm, clear down to his toes, trying to relax. It had been more than thirty-six hours since Al had made contact, and he was beginning to wonder if something had happened to him back at the Project. Laced through the worry for him was a thread of worry for himself, too. What was he going to do if Al never came back?

He had to think about it. A couple of times he thought he remembered Ziggy managed to get somebody else through to him, but the memories were spotty. It had never really worked well. He couldn't hear, or couldn't see, or something was always wrong. Al was his only sure link to the Project, to Ziggy. If Al was gone, he was going to spend the rest of his life as a half-Mohawk half-Polish bartender who didn't read much.

95

He could always have faith that God or Fate or Chance, Time or Whatever the hell was Leaping him around wouldn't allow him to be abandoned in the seventies, but . . .

But he'd gone over that and over that: There were limits to what Whatever could do. That was why he Leaped to begin with. Leaping was connected to his *doing* something. *Accomplishing* something.

Of course, the next question was *what*.

He could get some petty revenge on Whatever by playing music that hadn't been written yet, but he couldn't remember any. His hands softened on the keys. There was one tune he could recall, always: "Imagine." He played on, still musing.

There was still another problem, one he'd been avoiding thinking about since the first moment of his Leap in: Just how serious was Wickie's relationship with Rimae, and what was Sam Beckett expected to do about it?

He didn't need Al around to know what his Observer would advise him about that. For a tactical genius, Al could be very predictable sometimes.

He didn't know Rimae very well. He didn't have any strong opinions about her yet. He did know he wasn't going to sleep with her; he was Sam Beckett, and Sam Beckett didn't do that sort of thing casually. "Mr. Morals," Al had called him once. Well, he could live with that.

It might be a little difficult to explain to her; she thought he *was* Wickie. Of course, by the time he got through telling her about the cabin, he might not have to worry about Wickie's sex life any more. He'd seen enough of Rimae's temper to know that the risk of Wickie losing his job was now a little more than 43 percent. It wasn't that she was a bad person, really, but . . .

He sighed and got up, closing the keyboard cover. Surely there was a laundromat open on Sunday. Besides, he had to return the rug shampooer.

If only he'd Leaped in just to clean the rug.

CHAPTER
TEN

The jungle talked at night.

He could smell the dark—a heavy, wet, rotting smell, a smell of dead leaves and unwashed humans and snakes.

Snakes. The black snake that curled through the bamboo bars and flickered its tongue at him, promising death, teasing him. The little grey-green snake that slid through and touched the lieutenant on the leg—the bare leg, exposed through torn and decaying cloth—the leg tied down so the lieutenant couldn't move it away—just touched him, that was all—and the lieutenant cried, and whimpered, and died.

The snake looked at him next, and he looked back.

He couldn't move. Each ankle, each wrist was roped to the bars of the cage; his feet were bare, his clothing was no better than the lieutenant's.

It was hot. Wet. Suffocating. His skin itched with the salt of old sweat.

The snake hissed at him, rose up swaying.

The dead lieutenant turned his head toward him and cried, each tear a memory. The flesh of the dead man's face was dry against his skull.

The snake was sliding against his hip.

The lieutenant's face turned into the face of Sam Beckett.

Al Calavicci screamed.

"Al, sweetheart, what is it?"

He exploded into wakefulness, sweating, and Janna yelped as his fist connected with her shoulder. The sound shocked him from wakefulness into awareness. The room was dark, but he wasn't in the jungle. He wasn't tied. There was no snake. No lieutenant.

No Sam Beckett either.

Only . . . Janna, that was her name. Janna, who was backed up against the headboard staring at him, clutching at her shoulder. Janna, his wife. Who went from clutching her shoulder to touching his, lightly, seeking and giving reassurance at one and the same time. Ignoring her own pain to comfort his.

Late afternoon. A hotel room in Santa Fe, New Mexico. He knew where he was now.

He sat up wearily. "Oh, God. Janna, I'm sorry. I'm really sorry." He didn't try to touch her. He couldn't bring himself to touch her. He rubbed at his wrists instead, as if rubbing could eliminate the almost invisible scars that still remained there, could eliminate the feel of ropes and steel and restraint.

He went from rubbing his wrists to rubbing his temples, wondering how he was going to explain. It had been a long time since he'd had a dream like that.

"You've been dreaming a lot lately," Janna said softly, getting up.

He could see her, he realized. There was a light on in the bathroom, fading sunshine coming through the curtains. He was in a hotel room in Santa Fe, not locked up in a cage in Vietnam; and he could see her, silhouetted by the light, all curves and sleek lines and . . .

"What do you mean, 'dreaming a lot lately'? I haven't had those dreams in a long time."

She came back with a glass of water and a pair of pills. "Here. Take these."

"What are they?"

She expelled a long breath through elegant nostrils. "Al. These are the pills Dr. Beeks prescribed for you. They'll help you sleep without the dreams." Her tone was matter-of-fact, not impatient, not accusing. You have dreams. This will help. Here—take them. Feel better.

"I don't *have* dreams," Al said, forgetting momentarily what had awakened him in the first place. "What the hell is going on?"

But if he stopped to think about it, he could remember: He had nightmares, memories that came back to haunt him. And Verbeena Beeks was a psychiatrist, had been treating him for PTSD. Post-traumatic stress disorder: Flashbacks to Vietnam, and the six years he'd been a POW, most of those years trapped in a bamboo cage too small to stand up or lie down in, each limb tied to the interlacing bamboo bars. This dream wasn't even particularly bad, compared to some he'd had.

He rubbed his temples again and reached for the glass and pills.

"Okay." It wasn't easy to accept it. Apparently this version of his life had drawbacks as well as a wife.

He paused in the act of putting the pills in his mouth, wondering. Was Janna his sixth wife, or had he managed to skip a few divorces this time?

"Better close your mouth, you'll catch flies," Janna advised. The light from the bathroom, brighter than the sunlight, fell across his face, momentarily blinding him.

"Turn the room light on," he said sharply.

Saying nothing, she reached past him to turn on the bedside light. Its illumination drowned out the spotlight from the bathroom. Al closed his eyes and took a deep breath. "Okay. Thanks. Sorry—"

"It's all right, dear. I should have remembered about the light." She moved around the bed, sat down, began rubbing his back, kneading his shoulders. "You're worried. We'll go back first thing tomorrow. You need to talk to Sam, see that he's all right. Go ahead and take your pills, you'll sleep better."

He nodded. She was right, of course. He *would* sleep

better. The pills would give him sleep, without dreams. Without nightmares.

Without memories.

The lieutenant wasn't Sam Beckett.

He hadn't abandoned anybody. He couldn't have kept the snake from biting the other man; he couldn't have saved him. Calling out wouldn't help. He couldn't reach the lieutenant. Couldn't touch him. Couldn't help.

If he'd said that in a session, Verbeena would tilt her head and raise one eyebrow at him, waiting for him to draw the obvious conclusion.

But when he stepped back into the Imaging Chamber, the chances were good that Janna would be gone.

His memories of two distinct pasts were blurring.

He was leaning against her, her arms were around him, his head leaned back against her shoulder. She was comforting, saying nothing. She was a very patient woman, was Janna. He could . . . *remember* . . . her waking him from other nightmares in the recent past. He could almost remember how they met, at the first Project Christmas party. He could remember the first time he had touched her face, the movement of her cheek under his hand when she smiled at him, that bright, lovely smile.

He could almost remember a whole life with her, and they were good memories.

He set the glass aside and turned to hold her. He couldn't fall in love with her. He couldn't. He had to go back and help Sam change the past. The future.

The now.

He buried his face in Janna's hair and waited for the pills to take him back into the dark.

In the small, cluttered office in the back of the house down the road from the Polar Bar, Rimae Hoffman bent over the books, frowning as she riffled receipts in one hand and ran a calculator with the other. The locals weren't enough to pay the bills, even with Ladies' Nights and parties and every special event she could think of, even trying to peddle real estate on the side. Summer was always tough, but real estate and private parties usually provided a little cushion. This year neither seemed to be enough. It was starting out bad and she couldn't see any sign it was going to get any better.

What the hell had possessed Wickie to take back that quarter keg anyway? Something about kids, but that was bull—Kevin was of age, and that was all that mattered. Sure, it was only one sale, but what if the local kids decided to have the Midnight Hour bar down the road cater their parties? What if this sudden picking and choosing of his started applying to their parents? That could add up.

She ran her fingers through her hair and swore. She'd have to talk to him. And he'd better not depend on having slept with the boss to keep him out of trouble, either.

The trouble was she *liked* Wickie, she really did. The way he'd started acting recently, though, that was nuts.

She'd talk to him. He'd straighten out.

Maybe he could start playing the piano during his breaks from the bar. She hadn't known he could play—in the last ten months he'd never touched the instrument. But in the last two days his hands had moved over it as if they'd done it all his life.

An unconscious smile curved her lips.

Someone rapped at the back door, and she looked up, half in irritation and half glad of the excuse to put the receipts away. She could see the outline of a man through the amber glass of the top half of the door. She knew that shape. The smile came back.

He stood outside the door, waiting for an invitation—typical of Wickie. He'd wait out there forever until she came to let him in. Just standing there, looking up at her from the lower step—looking through the straight black lashes, almost shy, as if he wasn't certain of his welcome. She grinned at him and opened the door. "Well, I'm mad at you, but not that mad. Come on in."

And now he looked confused. She shrugged and stepped aside, and he entered, looking around the office as if he'd never seen it before—anything to keep from looking at her. If he'd had a hat in his hands, it would be turning around and around, his hands clenching at the rim.

But there wasn't any hat, and he had his hands shoved into his pockets instead. So she kissed him.

He jumped at first as if she'd jabbed him with a cattle prod, and then relaxed into it. He was actually getting interested, despite himself, when she stepped away again. "What's the matter?" she inquired. "Still not feeling up to par?"

"Oh, I'm fine. Really." He passed the back of his hand over his lips, as if he had to scrub away the feel of her in order to think straight.

She grinned at him. "Well, that's good news. It's about time. I was beginning to wonder if you were ever going to come at all."

He nodded, looking around. Stalling. He acted as if he'd never seen the place before, staring at the handmade curtains at the windows, the rag rug on the floor, the brown plaid sofa. He certainly ought to remember the sofa, she thought. They'd spent enough time there. Now he was acting like a shy kid, making her make the first move.

She had some new things on the walls, not pictures exactly, more like shallow window boxes made of wickerwork and pine cones. He studied them carefully.

He was still stalling.

"So what's the deal?" she said abruptly, tiring of the delay, irritated by his continued lack of responsiveness. Well, if that was the way he wanted to play it, fine. "Hey, if you don't have anything to say, I do."

"Why don't you go ahead then." He was being polite, she could tell, but he was also relieved that he didn't have to talk. Well, that was Wickie, all right. The strong, silent type all the way.

"Look, I don't want any more messes like you got into on Friday, okay? Just make the deliveries and take the money. Okay?"

He was looking directly at her now, and she wasn't sure she liked his expression.

"They're kids." The words were spaced out, precise. "A bunch of kids up by the river, getting drunk."

She shrugged. "That's none of our business. It was bought legal and paid for legal and it should be delivered legal. I'm in the business of selling liquor, not buying it back."

"But—"

"But nothing. I don't want to hear about this happening again, okay? Kevin's nineteen. He's legally a responsible adult. I'm not going to sell to somebody who's under age. I'm not that dumb—I don't want to lose my license. But I don't want to hear my head bartender has taken up Prohibition, either, or I'm going to have to find myself a new head bartender. Got that?"

He started to say something and stopped, seemingly baffled.

She shook her head, went over to the cabinet beside the stereo, and got out a bottle. "Here. *I'll* play bartender for a change."

"Isn't it kind of early?"

The laugh that escaped from her was more like a stifled chuckle. He really was nuts. "It's after four. I didn't think you cared."

He shook his head. "I'll pass, thanks."

Her lower lip twitched. "Suit yourself." She pulled a short, wide glass from the top shelf of the cabinet and poured an inch of whisky into it. "Confusion to the enemy."

The liquor was a shock going down, harsh against her throat. Despite what she might have told Wickie, she didn't usually drink this early. She gasped a little, clearing the fumes from her mouth.

Wickie was staring at her, as if something was slowly becoming clear to him, something he didn't like. It couldn't be the drinking; he'd seen her drink every night for almost a year.

"Fetal alcohol syndrome."

The words were spoken with an air of discovery, as if he'd finally pinned something down.

She choked, a trail of liquid dribbling out the corner of her mouth. Wiping it away with the back of her hand, she sputtered, "What did you say?"

"Fetal alcohol syndrome. Davey. The flattened aspect of the nose and philtrum, the space between his eyes, the autistic response. His mother was drinking while she was pregnant with him, she had to be. He has fetal alcohol syndrome. That's what's wrong with him. I've been trying to remember for the last two days."

She stared at him, unbelieving. This was Wickie? Wickie, who was pretty good in bed and knew a lot of oddball drinks but never got past the eighth grade? And who the hell was he to stand there with that look on his face, disgust and sorrow and—how dare he—*pity*—Davey!

She slapped the glass down on top of the cabinet, slopping liquid over her hand, ignoring it as it dripped on the wood, on the floor. "When did you become a doctor?" she asked mockingly. "Those are pretty big words for you, aren't they?"

He opened his mouth, shook his head as he changed his mind about whatever it was he was going to say. It gave her the chills. He wasn't *acting* like the Wickie she knew. "It doesn't matter. It's true, isn't it?"

"I don't know if it's true or not. I don't care. Davey's just as much a person as you are. What's this 'fetal alcohol syndrome' stuff anyway?"

"Use of alcohol by pregnant women has been shown to cause a range of defects in the developing fetus. There are plenty of cases in the literature."

" 'In the literature,' " she mocked, getting a little frightened. He sounded like some kind of rocket scientist or something, spouting off that way. "My, aren't we using big words these days?"

He came over to her, a quick panther stride, snatched the glass off the cabinet—it didn't slop for him, she saw

104

with growing resentment—and then he was holding it under her nose, and her resentment and fright began to boil over into anger.

"It doesn't have anything to do with 'big words,' Rimae. *This* is why Davey's the way he is. This is the whole reason, the only reason. Because his mother drank while she was pregnant! Didn't you know? Didn't anybody tell you?"

Even though she didn't feel threatened, he frightened her, and she got angry and slapped at his hand. The glass went flying, shattering against the wall. "Where the hell do you get off standing there telling me this stuff? Even if it is true, what difference does it make to me or Davey now?"

He stepped back from the intensity of her anger, back again as he saw her fighting tears, and that made her even angrier. "Get out of here, damn you. I don't know what you came over for, but I'm in no mood to listen to it now. Go lecture somebody else."

He couldn't find anything to say to that, which was just as well, Rimae thought, if he was going to stay employed at *her* bar. Her fingers curled around the glass of the bottle, pressed tight against the slippery, sticky surface. How dare he? How dare he? How dare he stand there with that look on his face, as if he was the only person capable of understanding *her son*? How dare he look at her with that mixture of accusation and compassion? She stared back and ground the glass into the innocent wood of the cabinet.

His shoulders slumped—his whole body seemed to shrink in on itself all of a sudden, as if he had been defeated somehow. He turned away without another word and went out the door, closing it quietly behind him.

She would not cry. She would *not* cry about something she'd lived with for sixteen years, ever since she found out that her lovely baby boy, whom she had chosen and loved with all her heart, was never going to grow up, not really. She had decided then, in that doctor's office, that it didn't matter. It didn't matter. She would take care of him just the way he was all his life, and she wouldn't even think about what Wickie had just said, wouldn't even think that it might be true. Rimae Hoffman had had plenty of things to cry about her life long, and she wasn't going to pick just one this late in the game. Davey was *hers*, and she never regretted it.

Past was past, and that was all there was to it. She'd take care of Davey, and Wickie Starczynski could mind his own damned business. And if he didn't, she'd fire his ass so fast he'd never know what hit it.

At the Project, Ziggy registered a change. Recalculated a percentage. Regarded it worriedly.

Something had to be done. Soon.

But what?

As the odds for Sam increased, the odds for Al decreased, and the computer that was the product of both of them hummed in discontent.

CHAPTER
ELEVEN

Gooshie hunched over the sports page in the Project cafeteria, absentmindedly munching a handful of tortilla chips as he scanned the scores. Little shards of baked white corn obscured the page, and he brushed them away impatiently. The cafeteria was filled with people taking a lunch break—it only held tables for thirty. The sound of conversation, eating utensils, and moving chairs made a blur of white noise.

Verbeena Beeks stood beside Gooshie's table, carrying a tray. "Good afternoon, Gooshie. May I join you?"

The Project's chief programmer peered up at her myopically and then heaved himself halfway to his feet. "Oh, Dr. Beeks. Of course. Please. Sit down."

Verbeena smiled and sat opposite him, unobtrusively brushing the detritus of his snack over to his side of the table. "How's it going?" she inquired, tapping the contents of a packet of creamer into her coffee.

Perhaps her tone was just that small bit too nonchalant; perhaps something else gave her interest away. In any case, Gooshie was no fool. He folded the newspaper away and thrust his head forward nervously. "It's going very well, Doctor. Why?"

"Oh, no reason." She smiled abstractedly at him, pretending far more interest in her packaged meal than it actually warranted. The little cafeteria had a couple of wall-sized refrigerators, well stocked with frozen dinners, and lots of canned goods, but haute cuisine was beyond the Project budget. Verbeena had chosen ravioli with meat sauce; she poked at the pasta and wondered whether she might not have been better off with clam chowder.

Or if she'd stayed in her San Francisco practice, she could be dining out on Pier 39, eating fresh Alaska salmon. Was salmon in season now? She couldn't remember.

Instead she'd taken on a professional challenge and landed in the middle of a desert in New Mexico, and she was eating defrosted ravioli under the anxious eye of a man who probably thought in binary.

Smothering a chuckle, she laid her fork aside and smiled at Gooshie. "No reason, really. Just asking."

"But you're a psychiatrist," Gooshie said.

"You sound like that joke about the two psychiatrists meeting and saying 'Good morning' to each other, and spending the rest of the day wondering, 'What did he *really mean* by that?' "

"Well, I was wondering."

"Don't worry so much, Gooshie." Gooshie was one of those people a junior therapist would have a field day with, pinning him down and asking him questions until the man's skin popped out with beads of sweat and his hands twisted around each other, wringing with terror. Verbeena, on the other hand, had Gooshie pegged as someone who was naturally nervous. He didn't need a doctor harassing him.

"Well, you don't usually sit with me."

"Nope, not usually. But I looked at my list this morning, and it said I'd had lunch with practically everybody else, so—" She grinned. "And besides, it was the only free seat in here. Give me a break, hon, I'm not a doctor all the time."

Gooshie grinned uncertainly and nibbled at his mustache, which was ragged from the habit.

"So how's the programming biz?" Verbeena inquired, giving the ravioli another try. If she concentrated, maybe she could pretend it was sole, covered with lemon sauce and capers. . . .

"Oh, it's fine, just fine."

"Made any progress on the problem?"

Gooshie looked away, his face turning red. "No."

"I didn't mean to make you feel bad," she said gently. "I was just hoping."

"It isn't right," Gooshie burst out. "Everything runs just fine. It doesn't make sense. If there was something wrong somewhere, it ought to show up in other programs. Everything's knit together. But everything's working the way it's supposed to."

Don't let Al hear you say that, Verbeena thought, smiling through a mouthful of overcooked pasta. As for the sauce—

Gooshie's hands wrapped around the plastic bag, twisting it, and the handful of chips left inside crumbled. He didn't notice. "We've gone through *everything,*" he said earnestly, as if Verbeena might not believe him. "Everything we can think of. There was that time that Ziggy was trying to add on to herself, years ago, and we thought that might be involved, but that all happened after Dr. Beckett Leaped, so that couldn't be it. We thought maybe she'd started earlier, but Dr. Beckett wouldn't have let her.

"And then there were those new chips he invented. I'm not sure what they might have done." Gooshie's eyes were magnified by his glasses. He'd never bothered with the surgery that would have made glasses unnecessary; too worried about things going wrong, Verbeena thought. Gooshie was always worried about things going wrong.

They rarely did in his part of the Project, but the one thing that *had* gone wrong was more than enough to make up for it. And Gooshie was sure it was all his fault, no matter how much he'd like to blame the neurochips Sam invented.

Verbeena was in no position to argue with him. All she could do was keep an eye on him, make sure that guilt, and the effort to locate the bug in the program, didn't drive him into a breakdown.

She finished her lunch, glanced at her calendar, and sighed. She needed a staff meeting, needed to look at performance review, wanted to talk to the compensation people about hiring a new doctor to work in the Waiting Room. The trouble was getting someone through the clearance process. A medical doctor who could undergo the kind of scrutiny involved in getting cleared for Project Quantum Leap usually didn't want to work there to begin with. It wasn't a particularly attractive place to work, off in the middle of the desert.

First, though, she needed to go look in on her most important patient again.

She nodded farewell to the chief programmer and put away the debris of her meal and stepped into the elevator to the depths of the Project.

The Accelerator, the Imaging Chamber, the Control Room, the Waiting Room were all together on a level about halfway down. Below them were the layers of computer offices, the cabinets that held Ziggy's mechanical guts, the lowest-level offices, Beckett's abandoned biochip laboratory. Verbeena never had occasion to visit the lower depths of the Project. Her concerns centered on the Waiting Room. She walked through the Control Room without even a glance at the large table of glowing cubes in many colors that occupied its center, or the glittering silver ball suspended in the air above it. She nodded at the technicians buzzing like flies around a rectangular box of Jujubes and kept going.

Pausing outside the door to the Waiting Room, she glanced up at the ceiling. "Ziggy? I don't suppose Al's come back yet?"

"No, Dr. Beeks."

Drawing a deep breath, she knocked lightly at the door, waited a moment, and walked into the white room with the hospital bed and the state-of-the-art monitoring equipment, the stairway and the office up in the observation deck.

He was lying on the bed, half-dressed, his fingers knit under his head, staring at the ceiling. She marched briskly over, picked up the chart and scanned it as she said, "Good morning, Mr. Starczynski. And how are we feeling this afternoon?"

The hazel-green eyes—familiar eyes—shifted to follow her. The cold, suspicious expression on the man's face didn't fit well, as if the face had never been shaped to accept it. "I don't know how *you're* feeling, Doc. *I'm* doing just fine."

It was Sam Beckett's voice. It had to be, coming from his lungs and his vocal cords, shaped by his palate and lips and tongue. But Wickie Starczynski would hear his own voice. That was what his mind was used to hearing, so that was what he'd hear.

It was a fascinating dilemma, this separation and mix-and-match of mind and body. Verbeena could never publish any of her observations, but she made her notes anyway. Most of her colleagues wouldn't accept the proposition that the mind could be separated from the body—from the brain—to begin with. That was the school of thought that didn't accept the idea of the soul, or God, either.

Verbeena smiled coolly and scanned the chart. Blood pressure still high, but otherwise healthy. It could be worse. She could still remember the time Sam had Leaped into a woman with an insatiable craving for Milk Duds, chocolate turtles, and Godiva chocolates. As well as German chocolate cake, Hershey's Kisses, and almost anything else containing theobromine. Sam's blood sugar level and cholesterol count had gone through the roof.

"I see you've been eating well," she remarked. The chart showed he'd been exercising, too. That was very good. It would help keep his borrowed body in condition.

"They feed good here. The booze isn't great."

"I've often noticed that myself." He must not be much of a cook, she thought, placing the chart on the end of the bed. "Any other problems? Can I get you anything?"

He looked up at her and smiled lazily. "What did you have in mind?"

If he flexes his pecs at me, Verbeena promised herself, *I'm going to show the tape at the medical section's Christmas party. I'll save it for when we get Sam back and torture him with it. See what happens when you're not in your right body, Dr. Beckett? Serves you right for not being in your right mind either. Oh please, please flex 'em.*

He didn't. But he did grin, a slow, lazy grin, and lay still, enjoying the survey. Verbeena hoped he couldn't tell she was blushing.

"Can't help you with the booze, hon," she said at last. "I just wanted to see how you were doing. We're still working on things. If you don't have any questions, I'll check back with you later."

She turned around briskly and marched up the steps to the observation deck, closed the door behind herself and reached for the window blanker. "Dave, what's the story?"

The nurse on duty, a burly Hispanic with tightly curled hair, shook his head. "He doesn't show any signs of disassociation, anomie, stress, or tummy upset, but when he shaves he still stops to look at his face. Touch it. He still looks down at himself. Usual pattern. But he just doesn't react. Seems to be perfectly comfortable where he is."

"Weird. Really weird." Not exactly a professional diagnosis, but it would do.

"Yeah." Dave was starting work on a dissertation in abnormal psychology. Ziggy did the lit searches for him; he read the articles. He wanted to study multiples. Since he couldn't use the patient in the Waiting Room, he'd have to leave the Project in a few weeks to continue his studies under one of Verbeena's former professors at Cornell. Verbeena wasn't looking forward to losing him.

"So what do you think?"

Dave shrugged. "Ziggy ran old TV sports programs for him for a while—he's especially interested in the karate

112

championships. He's been looking at some of the books. His profile shows a lack of self-esteem, a lot of insecurity, but he's a good kid. Too bad it isn't something in *his* life that will change."

"Isn't it, though," Verbeena muttered, looking at the monitor. Wickie was lying staring at the ceiling, doing nothing. "What a waste."

"Can't we do anything about it?" Dave asked hesitantly. He was itching to apply his new knowledge.

Verbeena had a few theories of her own. The two of them looked at each other, then at the Visitor in the Waiting Room below.

"He hasn't asked for therapy," Verbeena mused. "I wonder if an Ethics Board would consider this an experimental intervention."

"Just teaching? Counseling?" Dave asked.

She'd become a doctor to help people, Verbeena reminded herself. To make a difference. Abruptly, she grinned. "Why, Mr. Medina, I do believe you're right."

Elsewhere in the Project, a shadowy branch of possibilities began to take shape, as yet unconnected to anything at all.

CHAPTER
TWELVE

It was so obvious. How could he have missed it? All the physical signs were there, all the behaviors. He'd thought Davey was just challenged, the way Jimmy La Matta had been; whether it was retardation or autism, it would have been due to some genetic damage. Tragic, but hardly anyone's fault. The sensation of one of the holes in his memory abruptly filling in was almost physical.

He had to give a lot of credit to Rimae Hoffman. FAS symptoms ranged from imperceptible to incapacitating, but one of the most common was a short attention span. It couldn't have been easy, raising Davey. And if she'd taken in her niece as well, she must have a truly generous soul, no matter how incongruous her relationship with a bartender young enough to be her son might be.

He couldn't remember how much had been known about FAS in 1975, or more to the point, in the middle fifties, when Davey's mother had been pregnant with him. But it didn't matter. It was too late now. Nothing he could do could change things for Davey now.

Nothing. Not on this Leap.

Once again, frustration expressed itself in action.

He found himself walking, then jogging, then running along the sidewalk, his shoes slapping the concrete hard. He didn't know if Wickie was a runner. At the moment he didn't care. He had to get rid of the anger, the despair, the helplessness of finally figuring out what was wrong with a kid who wanted to fly and never would, and at the same time knowing there was nothing he could do to fix it.

His path took him down the main street of Snow Owl, around minor street repairs, up and down sidewalks, into the street when the sidewalks disappeared. He caught the green light at the intersection of Main and Ski Line Drive and kept going; even the red wouldn't have stopped him by then. Besides, there wasn't much traffic down by the auto dealership and pawnshop and pizza parlors, the delis and ski repair shops and boutiques so late on a Sunday evening, with the sun beginning to disappear and shadows slanting long and narrow in front of him, and he could push himself as far and as fast as he wanted, the mile through downtown disappearing under his feet.

Stabbing pains in his side weren't worthy of his attention, and after a while they went away. He kept on going, driving himself past a runner's wall and on into a new neighborhood and a second wind, Wickie's body answering his will, Wickie's lungs filling and contracting, Wickie's heart pounding in rhythm with Wickie's legs, running, running, uphill now, to the residential section of the town. No sidewalks here; he ran on the asphalt, dodging tree branches. Houses here were far apart, hidden at the end of narrow driveways leading from the road up into groves of trees, visible only from the lights that appeared in the windows. The shadows were gathering. The third time he stumbled, he began to slow down, and weariness hit him like a club.

Within six strides he was walking, holding his ribs, grimacing, hunched forward, gasping for air. He'd gone perhaps seven miles, he thought. Wickie was going to be really ticked off if Sam Leaped out right now and left the body for its rightful owner in this condition.

At least he was too winded to be angry any more. And now he had to walk all the way back.

Next time, he thought wryly, he should try to scream and

116

shout, or at least run in circles. That way he'd at least end up where he started from.

Well, he wasn't here to prevent Davey from suffering from FAS. He'd have had to Leap into Davey's unknown mother twenty years ago, and probably the Leap would have to have lasted the duration of her pregnancy—he shook himself convulsively. Once was enough, thank you; the thought of remaining in a woman's body for the duration of an entire pregnancy was almost enough to start him running again. He couldn't imagine how women did it. Over and over again, some of them.

Some things man was just not meant to understand.

So if it had nothing to do with Davey, what then?

And where the *hell* was Al Calavicci?

It was getting dark. The rare car that passed caught him in its headlights, spotlighting him like a deer and whizzing by, spattering him with the small stings of gravel and buffeting him with displaced air.

He could feel his heartbeat slowing down. Respiration was returning to normal. He thought about taking his pulse and decided not to bother. He seemed to be getting a lot of exercise this Leap, anyway. He wondered whether Wickie would be grateful.

He wondered whether Rimae would be, too. But he decided not to pursue that line of thought, since that seemed to be what was leading to all this sweating stuff. It wasn't the way he usually reacted, but then, he hadn't been himself lately.

Laughing hollowly, he trudged back up the road, back past the delis and ski shops and boutiques. He hadn't been himself for as long as he could remember, but with the state of his memory, that wasn't saying much, either.

If it wasn't Davey, and it wasn't Rimae, what was it? Kevin? Bethica?

Bethica?

He paused at the light, putting out a hand to support himself on the pole and using the other to scrub the sweat from his face with the hem of his T-shirt. About three more miles to go, he calculated. It might as well have been three hundred. He couldn't drive himself, or this body, any farther, not with any kind of speed. After a minute or two the panting stopped.

He couldn't seem to get a grasp on this Leap. He was doing a lot of sweating, and getting some music in, but that seemed to be about it.

Headlights spotlighted him again, and a truck pulled up beside him. He looked up to see Kevin grinning at him from the driver's-side window.

Oh, yeah. He'd been doing some fighting this time around, too. And it was beginning to look like he was going to be doing some more. He straightened up slowly as the truck pulled around the corner into the wrong lane, blocking his path, and the driver's door opened.

"Hey there, Wickie."

There wasn't anyone else in the truck, which surprised him. He wouldn't have expected Kevin to challenge him without an admiring audience. But audience or no, Kevin was getting out of the truck and facing him.

"Hey there, Kevin." He was glad he had his breathing under control, though the after-dark breeze of an early mountain summer was beginning to chill him. He wanted to keep moving. If he did, Kevin would interpret it as a victory.

He supposed he could live with that, but he wasn't sure Wickie could. But he didn't see any point in getting into another wrestling match with his self-appointed antagonist.

He stepped around the boy and started up the slope toward the Polar Bar. He wasn't particularly surprised when Kevin reached out and grabbed his shoulder.

"Where do you think you're going?"

Sam exhaled deeply. "I'm going home. It's late."

"You and I have something to settle first."

Sam still hadn't turned around to face the boy. "I thought we already settled it," he said. "Come on, Kevin. Haven't you done enough?"

It was the wrong thing to say; he knew it as soon as the

words were out of his mouth, but there was no way to call them back short of Leaping into himself in Wickie's body and putting right his own mistake. Which didn't seem too likely. Kevin's fingers were digging into his shoulders. Looking, he realized almost a moment too late, for the nerve center that would paralyze his right arm.

He dropped out from under Kevin's hand and took a long stride away.

"I'm not interested in getting into a fight," he said.

Instead of charging as expected, Kevin stood there and grinned at him. "You will be," he said. "Maybe not right now, but you'll be interested one of these days."

"You think so?"

"I know so. I don't forget." Kevin turned his back on Sam and paused, as if daring him to do something, and when Sam didn't take him up on the unspoken challenge he got back into the truck and started the engine.

"Real soon now," he shouted above the revving engine. "Wait for it."

The truck roared up Ski Line Drive, and Sam lifted his hand to protect his eyes from the gravel.

"You could at least have given me a lift," he muttered. "Kids got no respect these days."

He was beginning to sound like Al, he thought.

But where the hell *was* Al anyway?

Verbeena Beeks tapped the point of a pencil against the desk protector, sharp, hard blows just short of stabs. Her office, just off the Waiting Room, was painted an austere off-white, the same off-white that coated all the offices of the Project hundreds of feet under the ground. Verbeena had covered the plain background with oil paintings of fields filled with flowers, of barges in the canals of Venice. Al Calavicci called it her art gallery. He teased her about seeing patients in a museum.

She was the Project's senior medical staff member and had, in the current version of technobabble, "official oversight" of the Project medical team. Everything about the physical and mental health of the Project personnel was her responsibility.

She emphatically was not an expert in quantum physics or time-travel theory. Heisenberg's Uncertainty Theorem, as interpreted by Samuel Beckett, M.D. and multiple Ph.D., was a source of enduring frustration to her. She agreed in principle that the patient must be led to personal discovery of the self rather than simply being told, but . . . in this context, it meant that Al couldn't just come right out and *tell* Sam all about who he really was. Sam himself had set up an elaborate network of rules based on his own programming. It kept him in a state of chronic partial amnesia.

But that wasn't the key problem at the moment. It was second order at best.

Her key problem at the moment was Al Calavicci. Since Sam's only real link to his own identity was Al Calavicci, the Observer, linked to Sam through Ziggy the computer, Al was not only an Observer, but the focus to remind Sam of who he really was. It placed an incredible amount of pressure on him.

Verbeena had been about to suggest a little vacation to Al when Ziggy had notified them once again that Sam had found—or been placed in—yet another host, and the physical shell in the Waiting Room contained yet another Visitor.

Normally that news led to a carefully orchestrated series of events. Verbeena would make an immediate assessment of the Visitor. Al would enter the Imaging Chamber and Ziggy would center him on Sam. Simultaneously Ziggy would begin scanning history, looking for data on the individual into whose life Sam had Leaped, running projections on whatever it was that had gone wrong in that person's life, tracing possibilities of new histories predicated on changes Sam might effect.

All that had happened this time, too. But not even Ziggy could calculate the infinite consequences of seemingly minor changes, and Sam usually managed to screw up the most elegant of solutions. So Al needed to be there, on call; not only to reinforce Sam's sense of identity but to keep track of what he was doing.

And Al wasn't.

And it had been more than two whole days since Al's last contact with Sam. He'd made his initial contact, left the Imaging Chamber, and gone back to his office. The next day he'd taken a trip to Santa Fe with his wife. Ziggy, too, had been uncharacteristically silent on the question.

"Ziggy." Most of the time she looked up to that point at the ceiling she'd picked out as the "presence" of the omnipresent Ziggy. This time she stared straight ahead.

"Yes, Dr. Beeks."

"Do we have a problem here?"

"In what respect?" The computer was being careful. She hated it when Ziggy was careful. It generally meant trouble.

"In that Admiral Calavicci shows no signs of being interested in returning to his duties as Observer."

The computer didn't answer. Verbeena counted to one hundred, twice.

"Ziggy, don't you think this is a problem?"

"I can't provide guidance to Dr. Beckett without the intervention of the Admiral." The computer's voice was female, and at the moment petulant. If the computer had occupied a human body, it would be kicking something.

"So it *is* a problem."

"Of course it's a problem!" the computer snapped.

"Have you tried talking to the Admiral?"

"He's busy." Ziggy was definitely sulking. Verbeena could detect a distinct undercurrent of jealousy, and she stifled a smile.

Ziggy's visual sensors were sharper than she thought. "You're laughing at me."

Better watch it, Verbeena thought, *or I'm going to be back to psychoanalyzing the computer. I don't think I'm up to a virtual Electra complex today.*

"No, I'm not laughing at you," she prevaricated, groping for something else to be laughing at to divert the computer's wrath. "It's the Admiral. He certainly *is* busy these days."

There was a long pause before Ziggy answered, an unaccustomed hesitation. "He wasn't that busy before."

"No, he—" Verbeena paused, a small alarm bell having gone off deep inside. "Before what, Ziggy?"

An even longer pause, as if the computer wasn't sure it should speak. "Before the actualization of the present."

Verbeena blinked. "The *what* of the present?"

"The actualization." Now that Ziggy had made up its "mind," the computer was impatient, as it often was with mere human intellects. "Before the current present became real, when the Admiral wasn't married to Janna Calavicci. He was dating Tina—"

Now Verbeena was completely confused. "Tina Martinez-O'Farrell? Al dated the Chief of System Design?"

"Constantly," Ziggy confirmed.

A horrible suspicion was beginning to dawn in Verbeena Beeks. She tried to visualize Al with the tall, brilliant, idiotic-sounding redhead. On the one hand, it was patently ridiculous. On the other hand . . . it was all too possible.

"Are you saying the current reality isn't real, Ziggy?"

"No, Dr. Beeks. It is perfectly valid." The computer paused in a way she instinctively mistrusted.

"What aren't you telling me, Ziggy? What do you mean, Al dated Tina? Al's never looked at Tina."

"In *this* reality," the computer repeated patiently.

"You mean . . . in some other reality . . . he *did*? He cheated on Janna?" She'd kill him herself, she thought wildly, she'd . . .

"In other realities he was never married to Janna Fulkes."

That silenced her for several minutes. She gazed unseeingly at the sheaf of reports sitting on her desk, on the little ragged holes in the desk protector. At last she said softly, "Did I know about this, Ziggy? About Al dating Tina? In these—" It was hard to say. Hard to believe. "In these 'other realities'?"

"Of course you did." Ziggy sounded impatient. "Tina was your best friend on the Project."

"Tina—my best friend?" That thought alone was enough to boggle the mind. She couldn't imagine having enough in common with the Chief Design Engineer to have a conversation about. "And I know for a fact that Al Calavicci has never given her the time of day. . . ."

"*This* time."

Verbeena opened her mouth as if to protest, and then closed it again. She was trying to grasp the implications of what she was hearing, as well as the multiple definitions of "time."

"Ziggy," she said at last, "when did all this happen?"

"When the Admiral was last in the Imaging Chamber," the computer said. "It doesn't always happen that way, of course. Dr. Beckett can—and does—change the time line at any time. His being in the past is the first change to begin with."

Verbeena laid the pencil down, very carefully, and knitted her fingers together. "At any time," she repeated flatly. "So while we're talking here, he could change things?"

"That's correct."

The doctor stilled a frisson of fear. "And would I know? Would I be aware of the change?"

"No. Because the 'you' you would be in that moment would have a different history. Surely you realized this, Doctor. When Dr. Beckett puts things right, he changes the future. Not just for a particular individual, but for everyone that person touches. Changes . . . change things. For everyone. Everywhere."

For everyone? Verbeena wondered. *For me? Is Ziggy saying I'm different too?* The thought made her mind reel, as if the world around her had shuddered, settled into a slightly different, more awkward and definitely uncomfortable configuration. She couldn't accept it. If what the computer said was true, then nothing—*nothing* was dependable any more.

"Have you told me this before, Ziggy?" she whispered.

"Yes," the computer said softly. "Often."

Verbeena closed her eyes, took a deep breath.

Opened them again.

"How do you know?" she challenged. "Don't you have a new history too? How can you be aware that anything is different?"

"Because of the nature of the Project and whatever went wrong with it," the computer said, almost sadly, "I don't participate in time, Dr. Beeks. I observe it."

CHAPTER THIRTEEN

Sitting at the dining room table, moving the silverware randomly back and forth and down and up, Bethica heard the crunch of gravel, saw beams of light stab through the front windows and probe the gauze curtains as Rimae's station wagon pulled into the driveway. She sat unmoving, staring at the patterns in the grain of the maple table, listening to the sound of the engine being killed, the car door being opened. After a measurable pause the door slammed, and footsteps came up the walkway.

"Hey there, sweetie. Where's Davey? Is that dinner?" Rimae dropped a large purse beside the sofa in the front room, went to the liquor cabinet, and fixed herself a drink. She took a long swallow, looked at the glass, and made a face. "You'd think this stuff would taste better, wouldn't you?"

Bethica didn't look up. "Davey ate already. He's back in his room, looking at his Superman pictures."

Rimae gave her an odd look at her tone and sauntered into the kitchen. She glanced into the frying pan. "Looks good."

"It's all gunked up together," Bethica said. "I have to throw it out."

Rimae sighed and sipped. "I'm just batting a thousand today, aren't I?" she asked the ceiling. "Mother of the Year, that's me. Late again."

"It's okay, Rimae." Bethica got up and started rummaging in the cabinets for something to put the spaghetti sauce in.

"Well, did *you* eat, anyway?" Rimae asked.

She hesitated, glanced at the table with its betrayingly clean utensils. "Uh, I'm not really hungry."

Rimae took a last swallow of her drink and looked at her through narrowed eyes. "You sure about that, honey? You look a little peaked."

Bethica nodded, busying herself with the dishes.

Rimae sighed theatrically. "Well, okay. I'm too tired to argue about it. Besides, you're putting on some weight. I don't guess it's going to hurt you to miss one meal."

Bethica shook her head, agreeing, and went on scraping out the stainless steel frying pan. She'd gotten sick twice from the smell of frying meat. She was feeling nauseated again at the sight of the cooling sauce.

She couldn't get sick now. Rimae would figure it out in a second, and then all hell would break loose.

She couldn't keep it a secret forever. She needed to talk to Kevin, and she'd better do it soon. Maybe at the party tomorrow night; she could get him away from the guys, from Rita, long enough to talk to him. Tell him. Figure out what to do. He was a jerk, but he was smart. Besides, it was all his fault, really.

"Honey, I think I'm just going to go to bed, okay? I'm really beat."

"Sure. G'night."

Her foster mother's hand brushed her hair, and she gave her a quick peck on the cheek and left her there, staring at the table.

It was always this way. Rimae worked 'til late, and then came home. If she didn't go straight to bed she stayed up and did paperwork for the bar. She'd do the same thing tomorrow night, and Bethica would wait a half hour or so, go into Rimae's purse and get the car keys. She hated driving the station wagon, with its blue-and-white "Polar Bar" sign on the door, but she wasn't the only kid in the

126

regional high school who still took the bus to school. She wasn't one of the clique with their own cars, and she didn't date them. It was the dirt wagon or nothing.

So she'd get the car and drive up to the ski run and meet them up there, and she'd get Kevin alone and tell him, and then ask him what to do. What *he* was going to do.

She stared at her reflection in the bottom of the pan as suds slid down, at the blurred short brown hair and pale face and two great dark blue eyes, and sniffled. Her reflection blinked back at her, and she wiped at her nose with the back of her hand. It was such a stupid mess. She should be happy, having fun.

Not wondering what to do about a baby.

Kevin could tell her what to do.

He'd better.

His parents were rich. He was captain of the ski team, he was the smartest guy in school. He got all A's in calculus. He was going to go to USC in the fall. He was going to be an engineer and he was going to have a million dollars by the time he was thirty—he always told her so. If anybody else said that, she'd laugh at them, but not Kevin. Kevin Hodge really would do all those things, and be all those things. He'd have his own plane, and some really fast car. He'd live in a really great house, like the condos Bethica cleaned for the tourists during the season, like the big fancy houses they went home to in Chicago and New York and Beverly Hills. Not like this dump. He was *so smart.* . . .

And he was a jerk.

She had to tell him because he had a right to know, but the practical side of her nature knew that Kevin wasn't going to help at all, except maybe to give her some money for a quiet abortion, and she already knew she didn't want that. Even though he'd rejected her, driven her to do things she'd never considered doing before.

All in all, Verbeena thought, it was a most unsatisfying interview.

She'd love to be able to say to the man sitting across the desk from her, "Okay, bud. Either get straight with me or I'm going to yank your clearance, I'm going to make you talk to me—"

Al was leaning back in the chair, arms crossed across his chest, his stare cool and unwavering, and Verbeena recalled suddenly that he had faced worse interrogations than hers. Threats, especially threats she couldn't, wouldn't follow through on, would only increase his resistance.

So she tried the opposite tack. She surrendered.

Tossing her pencil onto the desk, she held up her hands. "Al, I don't understand. I don't understand the Project, I don't understand what went wrong. I don't understand why Dr. Beckett seems to be possessed at regular intervals by other people—"

"He *is* other people," the man across the desk interrupted.

Verbeena felt a small flash of triumph, quelled it before it could show.

Instead she heaved a large sigh.

"That's what you and Ziggy tell me, and a lot of the evidence supports you—electroencephalograms, physical responses, kinesic patterns, IQ tests. If it weren't for the little matter of DNA, retinal patterns and fingerprints, I wouldn't have any trouble at all believing you."

"Sam's mind Leaped. His body is occupied by the mind of the person he Leaps into." Despite himself, Al could not prevent a small gesture of one hand. *Mal'occhio*, Verbeena noted. The sign against the Evil Eye.

So it bothered him more than he liked to admit. She studied him curiously. "When you go into the Waiting Room, Al, who do you see?"

The abortive gesture again. "I see . . . I see Sam Beckett. I see . . . people." His arms sprang apart from each other as if they were like poles of a magnet, and windmilled. "I don't know how to tell you what I see. I look at Sam

128

Beckett's body and as soon as I look in his eyes I know, *that's not Sam*. I don't know who it is, but I know it's *not* Sam."

"We don't know how the brain organizes information so that we can look at pictures and know whom they represent," Verbeena said quietly. "We don't know how we can see a person as a child and recognize him as an adult. We don't know how we can tell the difference between two people, superficially similar, without conscious thought or decision—"

"I don't know either," Al said. "I don't care. I told you from day one, that isn't Sam in there. He's"—Al waved vaguely at the wall, the ceiling—"out *there* somewhere."

"And when you go into the Imaging Chamber and Ziggy centers you on Sam, what do you see?"

Al's eyes narrowed, and suddenly he was very calm and controlled again. He could tell where this was going, Verbeena realized.

Good. Let him.

"I see people. I see"—he paused, capitulated—"Sam." He rallied. "Why are we going over old ground, Verbeena? Are you working for the Senate now?"

She ignored the questions, pursuing her line of argument. "And you're the only one who can see Sam Beckett, aren't you?"

"Sometimes other people can," he protested feebly. "Kids can. Animals. Even you once."

"That's not really true, Admiral, and you know it. It takes more power than even Ziggy is capable of to allow me to see Sam, and even then—"

She paused and bit her lip, exhaling a long breath through her nostrils. She'd stepped between the disks of the Imaging Chamber, she'd seen—someone—once. Someone in torment. Someone Al had assured her was her friend, the Director of the Project, Samuel Beckett.

That person had looked more like an inmate of an insane asylum to her. A very poor, very primitive insane asylum.

And it was obvious that the man looking at her couldn't hear a word she was saying.

"Okay," Al said at last. "Okay. I know why I'm here." He fumbled at the inside pocket of his rust red suit jacket for a cigar, unwrapped and trimmed it with neat, economical, practiced movements, and bit down hard on it without lighting it.

"You want me to go back and make contact with him again." He looked her in the eye, defiantly.

"More than that, I want to understand why you're reluctant to do so." There was Ziggy's version, of course. She didn't want to think about Ziggy's version.

The Observer had broken eye contact as soon as the words were out of her mouth. He took the cigar out of his mouth and examined the chewed end as if there were something particularly interesting about it.

"Admiral, he needs you." It was the second time she'd used his title, in a not-so-subtle appeal to his sense of duty. He knew the gambit, and recognized its power over him. He wouldn't look at her.

"Al"—she was shifting from an appeal to duty to an appeal to friendship—"what's wrong?"

He wasn't really looking at the cigar, she realized suddenly. He was turning it over and over in his hands, drawing her eyes to it, but his own eyes were elsewhere. He was looking at his wedding ring.

As if he'd never seen it before.

"Ziggy was right," she breathed.

He glanced up then. "Ziggy? Right? Give me a break!"

"She was. She said, every time you went into the Imaging Chamber to help Sam change the past, the future changed too. And this time you don't want it to. It's *your* future, isn't it? It's your present. Your *now* that you're trying to preserve."

There was a long silence, and then the man sitting across the desk from her closed his eyes. "It's never happened like this before, Verbeena."

"What do you mean?"

He drew in a long, shuddering breath and looked down at the dark end of the cigar in his hands, the indentations where his teeth had clamped into it.

"Did you know," he said, so softly she had to strain to hear, "he once had the chance to save my first marriage? To Beth?" A sudden thought struck him, and he glanced up. "I *was* once married to a woman named Beth, you know."

"I know," Verbeena said. Of course he had been. Why would he think she needed to be told?

Then she realized why, and sat back again.

"He didn't do it. It was against the rules, he said. So Beth had me declared dead, and she got married to somebody else."

He smiled, and it was not a pleasant smile to see. "He's not perfect, you know, Verbeena. Oh, eventually he always does the right thing—that's what makes him Sam—but he's tried to break the rules a time or two for his own benefit. He's thought about it, at least.

"But he never knows—he's never even *asked*—what it does to us here. And that's why he made the rule in the first place, to protect the future from random changes in the past."

Verbeena bit her lip. Al's face was a study in resignation.

"You know, sometimes I step out of the Imaging Chamber and *Sam* is married? A dozen times, that's happened now. Not always to the same woman, either.

"Sometimes Tina and Gooshie are married, and sometimes Tina and I—" He paused, glanced up at her. "Ziggy says we're all kept in a kind of static globe, the same stasis that allows her—and me, of course, because of the link—to remember all the histories that happen and unhappen again. Except I'm only human, of course, so I can't keep things quite as straight as she can.

"For some reason, the Project never changes while I'm in it. Outside, it's probably changing all the time. I've even

131

seen it happen, when I'm in Washington." He laughed quietly. "You know, one time I came back and Tina was a blonde. Not even Ziggy could figure out how Sam caused that one."

"So it's true, then? The last time you went into the Imaging Chamber you weren't married to Janna?"

He let go a long breath. "Yes. I didn't even know who she was. Then."

It was the hardest thing Verbeena Beeks had ever done in her life. But it had to *be* done, and she was the one who had to do it.

She stood up, a tall angry black flame, and pointed at him. "Are you going to abandon Sam Beckett in the past for the sake of the present, Albert Calavicci?"

"I never said I wouldn't go!" He was sitting straight in his chair now, looking up at her, his black eyes snapping.

"But you're going to put it off, and put it off, until it's too late, aren't you? Until it's too late for Sam to change the past, to change *your* present! And what happens to Sam if you do that, Al? What happens to Sam if he fails?"

"We don't know! Maybe nothing! He hasn't always changed what we thought he would! It's all random! His Leaping doesn't *depend* on his changing things. . . ." He shut up abruptly, inhaled.

"Not the things you think he ought to be changing, anyway. Isn't that it, Al?" She sat down again, deflating into the chair. "He doesn't change the things we think he ought to, but we don't really know what God or Fate or Chance wants changed. We don't really know, ever, what tomorrow is supposed to look like. Do we?"

The two of them stared at each other. "The question really is, is it supposed to look like today?" she finished. "And what are you going to do about it, Al?"

MONDAY

I have done one braver thing
 Than all the Worthies did
And yet a braver thence doth spring
 Which is, to keep that hid.
   —John Donne, *The Undertaking*, **st. 1**

CHAPTER
FOURTEEN

Sam was getting tired of waiting. On Monday, according to the rota tacked to the corkboard behind the bar, he was scheduled to work from eleven to three in the afternoon and from eight until midnight. He spent the morning working on the broken windows of the cabin, making a list of the people he'd met and what he knew about them. It was something like trying to identify the suspects in a murder mystery, with all the motives, before the murder was even committed. He wished he had a better idea of what the future was supposed to look like.

But since the future wasn't putting in an appearance, he decided to try it on his own. Pulling on a pair of heavy work gloves he'd found in one of Wickie's dresser drawers, he picked out the broken glass with a pair of needle-nose pliers. He'd gotten new panes of glass, cut to specification, the first thing that morning. Then it was just a matter of picking out dried putty and old glazier's points, cleaning out the rabbet, doing a little sanding and painting. While he waited for the paint to dry he chewed thoughtfully on a straw, staring into the trees, and started mentally sorting and organizing.

There was Kevin, the first person he'd met on the Leap. He was just a kid, but he was obviously a leader to the local teens; he was the one buying the booze. He had a very nasty streak in him. What could go wrong in Kevin's future?

Anything or nothing, he had to admit. If he racked his memory, he could recall that he'd known a lot of kids who'd had beer parties in high school. Some of them had become upstanding citizens. Some of them were dead. He decided to leave the question of Kevin open.

Rimae Hoffman. His eyes narrowed. Wickie had a relationship with her, an "arrangement" Al would say, but it clearly didn't interfere with the employer-employee relationship. Rimae was a tough lady.

Bethica? She kept turning up in the oddest places. He'd seen her at the kegger with Kevin and the others, and what was she doing around Wickie's cabin last night—looking for her wannabe-Superman foster brother? Did Bethica have something else in her life about to go wrong?

Maybe he was here to prevent Bethica's baby from turning out like Davey. Was he going to spend the remaining months of Bethica's pregnancy following her around, making sure she didn't go drinking with her friends?

He didn't think so. Leaps didn't work that way. Of course, it wasn't a bad way to spend his time while he was waiting to figure out what else to do.

Who else?

Something in Davey's life, maybe?

He doubted it. Davey was mildly retarded, with an IQ somewhere in the low seventies. On top of that he was emotionally disturbed, belligerent, indifferent to instruction, discipline, or correction. Through no fault of his own, he was probably going to spend the rest of his life pushing a broom around a barroom floor, or something no more challenging. If he wasn't lucky, he'd spend time in jail for fighting. His chances of addiction to drugs or alcohol were high. His life expectancy was two-thirds that of Wickie Starczynski.

And for the life of him, Sam couldn't think of anything anyone could do to change what had gone wrong for Davey. Oh, Rimae could put him in a halfway house, arrange for supervised care for the rest of Davey's life, but for all Sam knew, she'd already made those arrangements. She certainly wasn't going to welcome any suggestions from him about it.

He sighed and examined the chewed end of the straw. Somewhere, in the lives of one of these people, something was going to go wrong. It was something that could change, something he could make right, something that could make a life better than it would otherwise have been. The wreck?

But how was he supposed to know what that something was all on his own? He was supposed to have an Observer. They were a team. He couldn't do this job by himself. God or Fate or Chance or Whatever had set things up in such a way that he had to work with a partner, and it wasn't fair for G or F or C to take that partner away from him.

He was feeling extremely sorry for himself, in fact, and he knew it. He was also feeling helpless. And angry.

The paint was dry. Taking a strip of glazing compound, he rolled it between his palms to make a thin rope, set it, installed the glass in the windows, reset the points, and finished off with more compound, neatly trimmed. There. His father would be proud of him. There was still *something* he could do right.

He supposed he could call everybody in Snow Owl all together in a room and tell them all to straighten up and fly right—and where did *that* phrase come from, anyway?— but they'd probably vote to have him put away.

And that wasn't funny even as a joke.

His nose was itching. He rubbed at it, wondering what was going to happen next. Something had to.

Something rustled in the pile of old leaves and young grass under the trees, and he stood up to get a better look. It rustled again. Not a snake, he thought. Squirrel, maybe, or raccoon . . . He walked over to the tree.

A grey face with huge yellow eyes peered up at him worriedly, and he sneezed.

The kitten levitated, bounced off his upper leg, and hit the side of the tree running. She paused at his eye level, her legs embracing the trunk, and stared at him, ears sharply forward, the whiskers around her nose and over her eyes quivering.

Her nose was a dusty pink. Her tongue, stuck out briefly to wash it, was brighter. Sam laughed under his breath, and the kitten tensed, ready to climb higher.

"Hey there," he said softly. "It isn't you, is it? There isn't something I'm supposed to do for you?"

The kitten opened her mouth for a soundless mew. Sam wasn't sure whether that was agreement or criticism.

"It wouldn't be the first time," Sam went on. "Sometimes animals need things to go right, too."

This time the kitten was definitely agreeing.

Sam's nose still itched.

"I don't suppose," he said, cautiously raising his hand to rub his nose again without alarming the cat, "that *you'd* know where Al is, would you?"

He couldn't help himself. He sneezed. Whether it was the force of expelled air or general panic, the grey cat leaped away, disappearing into the woods.

Well, it was *possible* he was here to fix things for the cat, but his medical background ran to humans, and he suspected the kitten wasn't old enough to need the attention of a veterinarian yet anyway.

He turned to find Rimae standing at the door to the cabin. She was watching him thoughtfully, one hand on her hip, one foot propped up on the step.

"What the *hell* is wrong with you?" she asked, her tone conversational. "Standing there talking to trees. Got all the windows in your house broken out. Lecturing me about things that weren't my fault, or your business. You're supposed to be helping me misspend my middle age, for cryin' out loud."

Sam couldn't think of a good response to any of it; the better part of valor was definitely discretion. "Somebody's been overfeeding your cat," he said at last.

"That damn cat's still hanging around here?"

"She's not yours?"

"Do I look like somebody who would own a damned cat?"

Sam had met any number of perfectly pleasant women who owned cats. He wasn't about to argue their merits with Rimae. Besides, he wasn't sure she meant it anyway. "Well. I mean, I thought she was yours."

Rimae shook her head, laughing. "Wickie, honey, you are *possessed*."

How right you are, Sam thought.

"Now you want to explain to me about these windows?"

She wasn't going to come to him. He had to go to her, crossing the little clearing, walking past her to open the cabin door. *If anything will make Al show up, it's this.*

She followed him in, looked around, sniffed at the lingering odor of ammonia and cleanser. "You cleaned the place up."

"It needed it."

"That much?"

"It really, *really* needed it."

"Hmph." She turned in place, noting the shampooed rug, the gleaming furniture, the scrubbed-down walls, the missing pictures, the lack of clutter. "You want to come do my place?"

"I don't do windows."

"Oh yes. The windows. Tell me about the windows, Wickie."

"They, uh, got broken."

"I can see that. I hope you weren't having a party without me." She walked over, checked the molding. "Nice job. I didn't know you knew how to do this."

He shrugged. "I wasn't sure I knew how to do it, either," he said. He didn't even have to mentally cross his fingers for that one; "window replacement" was buried in one of the potholes in his memory. He'd surprised himself, knowing what to buy and how to use the materials.

"How did it happen?"

"I have no idea," he said with absolute truth.

She stepped up close to him, walked her fingers up his chest and tapped one red fingernail on his chin. "No idea in the world, huh?"

"Not one," he said with false heartiness, stepping away. He raised one hand to wave to Bethica, who was walking past the cabin on the path through the trees.

Rimae shot the retreating teenager a sour look. "That kid needs to find a hobby." Her finely penciled brows knit together. "What the hell got into you yesterday?" she asked, changing the subject. "Are you out of your freaking mind?"

"No." The interruption allowed him to find something else to occupy himself; he got down on one knee, looking up at her while he cleaned rapidly drying compound off the blade of the putty knife, wiping it against the edge of the can. "I told you the truth about Davey. His mother drank when she was pregnant. And it affected him."

She shook her head. "What is it with you, honey?"

"I'm just not feeling myself lately." *Mom would be so proud of me,* he thought ironically. *Always tell the truth, Sam, she used to say, and shame the devil.* He stood up again. It was a mistake.

Rimae stretched up on tiptoe and kissed him. He caught at her arms—in case she wobbled—and returned the favor, to be polite. *Mind your manners, Sam, and manners will mind you.*

Mom, do you mind? he thought desperately at his memories. Sometimes his memories were rather inconvenient, especially at times like this. He didn't know what was worse, Al the hologram trying to coach or Mom the memory sitting back and looking motherly.

Rimae pulled away.

"I still don't know there's anything to that. You can't prove it. No one can. I don't know who Davey's mother was, so there's no way to know."

140

"I suppose not." There was no point arguing with her. It was too late anyway. He looked down the path, hoping he could catch a glimpse of Bethica. In case that wreck *was* going to happen, he still needed to keep her from going to the party tonight; still needed to keep her from driving back, getting into an accident, ending up a paraplegic. It was sometimes difficult to keep track of what he was supposed to be doing on a Leap, especially when Al wasn't around quoting odds all the time.

In any case Rimae was settling back on her heels, her fingers still entwined behind his neck. "Wickie, sweetheart, your heart just isn't in this. How about you go get ready to work and we'll talk about this again tonight when you get off from the second shift."

"Uh, that's going to be pretty late," Sam mumbled.

"It'll give you lots of time to think up a way to apologize for upsetting me, won't it?" She stepped away, tapped him on the nose again, and left him standing there staring after her.

"I guess it will," he mumbled. She turned the corner, moving out of sight, and he took a deep breath and turned to the trees, following Bethica, the one he might be intended to save.

She was waiting, as he suspected, hovering behind an oak tree near the stream, nudging a twig into the flow of the water. Leaps worked that way sometimes, as if God or Chance or Fate tried to give him a break when it could.

"Bethica?" He paused a few feet away. "I guess you heard all that. About Davey, and his mother drinking, and everything."

"I heard." She was looking at the ridge of mud on the toe of her sneaker.

"I know it's hard to understand," he offered. "It doesn't make a lot of sense. And I don't want to preach to you, but your baby. . ."

A wing of brown hair sheltered her face. She hunched a shoulder, building a barrier between them, and he wondered what was going through her mind. When she finally spoke, he had to strain to hear her. "You party."

It was true. Wickie drank. So did Sam Beckett. He wished he could promise Bethica that Wickie Gray Wolf Starczynski would stop drinking, would provide a role model for Bethica and Kevin and all the other restless young people of Snow Owl. But he couldn't; he wasn't Wickie, he was Sam Beckett, and if he did what he was supposed to do, he'd Leap out soon. He couldn't make promises and leave other people to keep them.

"You don't have to make the mistakes I make," he said at last.

"Do you really think Davey's the . . . the way he is because his mother had a drink while she was pregnant with him?"

"I think she had more than just one, but yes, that's the reason why. It's called fetal alcohol syndrome."

"You're making it up. You sound like Rimae. She keeps telling me not to party too, but she drinks. She owns a bar! And she knows I hang out with Kevin."

"She wants you to be better," Sam said helplessly. "I want to make sure you never have a baby like Davey—"

"It's not Davey's fault!" she said.

"Bethica, that's the whole point! It *isn't* his fault! It isn't a disease, it isn't genetic, it isn't anything but alcohol passing through the placental barrier and damaging developing cells so they can never be repaired. There isn't any cure for Davey or thousands like him—"

She was staring at him, eyes wide. "You're nuts."

He wasn't nuts, but he was preaching. And preaching, he well knew, only turned people off. It certainly hadn't impressed Rimae.

"Bethica, look. Promise me you won't go to that party tonight. That's all. Don't tell me you won't drink for the rest of your life. Just don't go tonight."

"You're nuts," she repeated. And turned, and ran away, leaving him standing.

"Now what?" he muttered. "I can't do anything right on this Leap." Out of habit, as much as anything else, he added, "Now what do I do, Al?"

"Beats me, kid," came a familiar voice from behind him. He spun around and caught himself on the trunk of a tree. There, standing in the doorway to the cabin, cigar in one hand and handlink in the other, familiar in snap-brim fedora and loud suspenders, stood Al, looking inexpressibly weary.

CHAPTER
FIFTEEN

He was barely able to contain himself until he got into the cabin, out of sight of witnesses. "Where have you *been*?" he burst out, torn between relief and outrage at having been abandoned. "I've been waiting for you for *days*. I thought something might have—" and then he got a good look at his friend, and his own feelings went into a skid. "Al? What's wrong?"

Al shook his head, raised one hand in a waving-away gesture. A puff of smoke hung in the air around Al's head, a smoggy halo from the ever-present cigar. "Never mind." He looked around appraisingly. "I like what you've done with the place. . . . What *have* you done with the place?"

"I cleaned up a little." Sam wanted to ask a dozen questions, and Al wouldn't meet his eyes. After elaborately surveying the living room, Al inspected the kitchen, stuck his head in the bedroom and bathroom, came back out again and made a great show of examining the handlink.

The silence between them stretched. Sam watched, bewildered, not sure what to say.

At last he fell back on business. "So, uh, has Ziggy figured out what I'm supposed to do on this Leap?"

Al's lips compressed, as if he was biting back a sharp retort, and he jabbed at the buttons on the handlink. "There's a girl—"

"Bethica."

Al's head jerked up and his eyes burned. "Already figured it out, have you?"

"No." Something was wrong, badly wrong.

Al continued, "It seems we were right all along about the wreck. She's going to go to that party up on the mountain tonight. On her way home she gets into a car wreck and ends up spending the rest of her life in a wheelchair."

"So much for theory." After all that time spent trying to figure out what he was supposed to change—"Does Ziggy have any suggestions about what I'm supposed to do?"

"You seem to be doing just fine as it is."

Sam had had enough. "Al, what's wrong?"

Al opened his mouth to answer and shut it again, shaking his head. "Nothing. It's nothing."

"Like hell it's nothing. You disappear for three days and when you come back you're snapping like a dog with a sore paw—"

"Colorful. Real colorful."

"You're ticked off at me for some reason, and I don't even know why."

Al sighed. "Okay, okay. It's not your fault. You can't help it."

"Help what?"

"Changing things."

Sam felt like a fish yanked out of water, his mouth gaping. "Al, I hate to remind you, but I'm *supposed* to change things. That's the whole point. It has been for years. So why are you all of a sudden so upset about it?"

"You never even think about it," Al burst out. "You blip around from one life to another, bim, bam, fix something here, change something there, and you never even think about the consequences—"

This was so blatantly unfair that Sam would have taken a swing at the other man if he'd had any hope of connecting. "I never think about the consequences? What are you talking about? I spend every minute of my *life* thinking about

146

consequences! Consequences are all I've got!"

"And now they're *my* consequences!"

"Yours? What do you have to do with it?"

"I don't know! You're the genius, you figure it out!"

There was another pause while Sam tried to figure out how the conversation had gotten so completely out of hand and Al chewed ferociously on his cigar.

"I don't understand," Sam said at last. "I'm sorry, Al, I don't understand." He shook his head. "I don't know what I did."

"I guess you don't." Al looked at the handlink again. "Ziggy says the accident happens late at night, when she's on her way home. If she doesn't go to that party, that should take care of it."

He was still angry, but his body language and tone conveyed clearly that he was setting aside his personal feelings in order to get the job done. The subject was changed, the dispute was closed. It was thorough and professional and subtly insulting, and it was treatment Sam Beckett had never received from Al Calavicci in all the years they'd worked together.

Al was his best friend, and he didn't understand. But if that was the way Al wanted to play it—

"Then all I need to do is talk her out of it."

Al, scanning the handlink, snorted. "It's not likely to be that easy. Ziggy says Bethica's going to talk some kid out of—" He whapped the little mechanism and stopped, staring at the information feeding across to him. "Give me that again, Ziggy."

The handlink squealed and blinked, colored cubes lighting up in sequence. Al tapped in a new series of codes, seeking a different answer and not getting it.

"What?" Sam circled behind the other man, trying without success to see what was going on with the glowing assemblage of cubes in Al's hand. "What is it?"

When he looked up and around at Sam, he was pale, and no vestiges of resentment or anger remained in his bright brown eyes. "Sam—she doesn't know it yet, but she's going to go to the party to try to convince a kid named Kevin not to kill Wickie Starczynski."

"Ziggy," Verbeena said to the empty air.

"Yes, Dr. Beeks?" The response didn't move the air as the spoken words of a physical presence would have. There was no sense of another person answering her.

Verbeena had never quite gotten used to it.

"Ziggy, tell me about Janna Calavicci."

The pause that ensued was uncharacteristically long, even for Ziggy, who had been programmed to include pauses to make its conversations more human. Finally, the computer answered, "The personnel files currently identify Janna Fulkes Calavicci as a personnel specialist who was hired into the Project in 1993."

"When did she and Al get married?"

She knew the answer. She had the personnel file on the computer screen in front of her. She knew exactly how Janna Fulkes had done in her performance ratings, how much she'd been paid, what days she'd taken off sick.

She knew Janna and Al's wedding day, not only from the file but from her own memory. She'd *been* there. She'd stood with the other women, Janna's friends, and tried to catch the bouquet. She'd had two pieces of wedding cake, carrot with cream cheese icing. She'd cried to see Janna and Al dancing their first dance as man and wife.

"Ziggy, Al tells me that before he last went into the Imaging Chamber he'd never met Janna. Never married her. He says you'll back him up on this."

Another long pause.

"Admiral Calavicci is correct."

Verbeena rubbed her eyes. "Could you go over that again slowly?"

"Ad-mir-al . . ." Ziggy's voice, a light soprano, deepened to baritone as the computer slowed down its speech.

"Ziggy, stop that. You know what I mean."

"Yes, Doctor." The soprano was back. "While the Admiral is in the Imaging Chamber, the changes effected by Dr. Beckett's presence in the past are potentials in this sphere, in our own present. When the Admiral returns—leaves the Imaging Chamber—he actualizes the change. In effect, he is carrying those changes with him into our present."

It sounded familiar, but—"He said he'd actually seen changes happen when he was in Washington. If he's carrying the change with him, how—"

"Those are changes outside the confines of the Project itself, Doctor. For a change to take place within this area—where I am—the Admiral has to trigger it. The same phenomenon which allows me to stand outside of Time to observe is disturbed by the Admiral's triggering of the Imaging Chamber and the link to Dr. Beckett. I can't maintain the integrity of the Project under that stress. They're part of me, after all."

It was almost the same conclusion she'd come to on her own. She swallowed. "So while he's married to Janna right now, as soon as he comes out again he won't be?"

"He *may* not be," the computer corrected.

"Well, is he or isn't he?"

"You mean, will he or won't he." Ziggy had a pedantic streak. "There's no way to know which possibility will become real until it actually happens. I can track what Dr. Beckett is doing, but I don't have the capacity to track every person his actions touch, plus every person their resulting actions touch. Nor can I always tell which of his actions is the important one. Futures are infinite possibility trees, Dr. Beeks. All we can see is the result when the Admiral leaves the Imaging Chamber."

"That's ridiculous. If that's the case, how can you and Al tell when Sam's succeeded in making the change he needs to make?"

"Because I'm not tracking all the repercussions. I'm only looking at the gross changes, the effects of a given action on one or two people. The subtle changes, however, will make greater or lesser changes like ripples in a pond, and we see those when the Admiral returns."

"So we're different every time the Admiral comes back?"

"Not necessarily," the computer said, an edge of impatience in the mechanical voice. "Not every change affects us every time. Other changes may damp out the effects.

"We do know that no matter what change is made, the Project must still have been created. Otherwise an unacceptable paradox would exist."

Verbeena couldn't help it. She laughed. " 'An unacceptable paradox'? Do you have any idea how that sounds?" And then she thought about how *she* sounded, arguing with thin air, and laughed again. "Ziggy, honey, you may be the wave of the future, but this whole business is crazy."

Somehow Ziggy managed to sound mortally offended. "If you say so, Dr. Beeks."

"I wish I knew how Sam programmed all those emotions into you," Verbeena said softly, shaking her head. "That boy could have made a fortune as a psychologist."

"Could you explicate, Doctor?"

"Ziggy, the only emotion he left out of you was the one nobody's ever been able to figure out. He knew enough about jealousy and anger and loneliness and pain and all the things that torment the human heart that he could put them into a program so a computer could feel them too, and you'll never know how much of an achievement that is."

"Which one did he leave out?" Ziggy demanded. "He didn't leave out anything!"

"Oh yes he did," Verbeena said softly. "Nobody's ever been able to program love, Ziggy."

It was a good exit line, and Verbeena took it, leaving the office and shutting the door behind herself with an emphatic, soft click.

"There was another emotion he left out," the computer said to the empty room. "He left out hate."

After a moment the computer answered itself. "That's because *he's* never understood that one."

CHAPTER
SIXTEEN

Sam polished the bar with a rag, occupying himself with busywork. There wasn't anyone in the bar yet. Except Al.

"Don't they have waitresses here?" the Observer asked. A strange expression crossed his face, as if he couldn't believe he'd said such a thing. Sam looked at him quizzically. What was so unusual, after all, in Al wondering where the women were?

"I think so," Sam said. This Leap was strange in more ways than one: First he couldn't get Al to show up; now, it seemed, he couldn't get rid of him. Not that he wanted to get rid of him, he chastised himself. But it was still strange. "The place doesn't serve food, so it doesn't attract much of a lunch crowd." The dusty bowls of pretzels on the counter certainly couldn't count as food.

Still, on the off chance someone might come in the door and be attracted to petrified pretzels, he collected the bowls and emptied them into the trash. Surely there were fresh supplies somewhere in the back room. At least digging them out would give him something to do besides polish the bar.

"So what are you going to do?" Al asked, walking through the bar to inspect the bottles lined up against the mirror. "What kind of place is this, anyhow? Never heard of some of these brands."

151

Sam's answer, reverberating in the cupboard in which he'd stuck his head, echoed oddly. "I guess I'll figure out something."

"Like what?"

The answer echoed too, and Sam pulled his head out and looked around to see Bethica pulling herself up on a barstool, with Al standing next to her, eyeing her judiciously.

"I thought I heard you talking to somebody, but there's nobody here," Bethica said.

"There's me," Sam and Al chorused.

"So were you talking to yourself?"

"Not exactly." Observer and Leaper exchanged glances and half-smiles over the girl's head.

She twisted around to look over her shoulder to see what Sam was looking at. To her eyes, there was no one there; from Sam's perspective, she was looking Al straight in the eye. Al was disconcerted.

Sam was amused.

But there was business to get to, and this was a good opportunity. "Hi," he said cheerfully. "What'll it be? Although I don't think I can serve you anything except—" he glanced around—"maybe ginger ale."

"Ginger ale would be great," she answered, turning back around again. "Where are the pretzels?"

Sam, caught in the act of removing the cap from a green glass bottle, raised an eyebrow.

"Well." Filling a glass with ice, he poured the amber liquid over it, added a straw and pushed the glass over to her.

Bethica sucked noisily on her straw.

Sam poured a ginger ale for himself and rested his elbows on the bar across from her. "Have you thought about what I said about the party tonight?"

Bethica nodded nervously.

"You don't have to go, you know." Out of the corner of his eye he could see Al watching the handlink, shaking his head. That meant his arguments weren't going to have the desired effect. He wasn't sure which effect Al was looking for—prevention of Bethica's accident or Wickie's death. Either one was something he'd rather not see happen.

He decided to try another tack. "Bethica, have you ever driven a car while you were drunk?"

The girl gave him an exasperated look. "Is this going to be another lecture? 'Cause I really don't want one."

"No, it's not a lecture. I just asked you a question."

She shrugged and concentrated on her drink, looking uncomfortable. "Yeah. But so have you!"

Wickie drove drunk. Terrific.

"I never said I was smart."

"Genius, yes. Smart, no," the Observer sniped.

Sam couldn't tell if Al was joking or not. "I never said it either," he protested to them both. Neither one seemed to believe him.

"Well, gee, you don't have to sound so mad," Bethica observed.

"Yeah, Sam. Don't get so thin-skinned. It's not your fault you're a genius." Al could never resist a free shot, knowing Sam was limited in his responses. Bethica didn't know Al was there; if Sam started answering Al, she'd think Sam had lost his mind. Sam was beginning to feel he had, anyway.

Sam closed his eyes, took a deep breath, and exhaled through his nostrils, trying to bring things back into focus. "All I'm saying is that you could get hurt that way, and I'd hate to see that happen." He sneaked a glare at Al. *You could get hurt one of these days too if you keep it up*, his unspoken message said. Al only smirked.

Bethica, for her part, glanced up quickly. "Really?"

"Really." Encouraged by her sudden lightening of attitude, Sam smiled. "You know, you probably shouldn't drink at all. Even if you weren't—" He paused.

Bethica's face went very still. "You still think I'm a little girl."

"Not so little," Al remarked.

"No, I don't think you're a little girl."

"And stupid," she muttered, poking at the ice in her glass with the straw. "At least, that's what you thought—"

"Well, yes, if you want to put it that way," Sam said, interrupting. "When a person gets drunk they sometimes don't know what they're doing. They get involved in things they never meant to—"

"Stop it! Just stop it!"

He was startled to see tears glistening in her blue eyes. "I'm sorry."

"I'll bet!"

Sam drew breath to answer and let it go again. He'd done it again. It didn't take much imagination to figure out what had been going on when Bethica got pregnant. Now she was looking at him as if he'd slapped her.

Al was watching him steadily now, waiting to hear what he was going to say next with as much interest as the teenage girl in front of him.

He was saved by the chirping of the handlink.

Al studied the readout and said nothing. Sam raised an eyebrow. Al ignored him.

"Look, if I asked you straight out, would you promise not to go to that party tonight?"

She looked up then, eyes blazing, and snatched her hand away. "You know, you're just as bad as Kevin is. You treat me like I'm some kind of little kid, unless it's convenient. Well, you can't tell me what to do!"

"Bethica—"

She slipped off the stool and walked out, slamming the door behind her.

Sam looked helplessly at Al.

He sighed and resumed polishing the bar. "Well, Plan A didn't work. Got any suggestions for Plan B?"

Now it was Al's turn to shake his head. "You could try taking Kevin out before the party."

The polishing rag paused. "Seems to me you've made that sort of suggestion before. It didn't work then, either."

"So sue me."

"Are you going to tell me what's going on, or are you just going to hang around forever making me crazy?"

"First you complain because I'm not around. Now you want to get rid of me?"

The rag slapped onto the bar, splattering water the length of the bar. "Dammit, Al, what is going on? Is it something at the Project? What's wrong?"

Al studied him, his face impassive, no emotions showing. It was the face of a man who had faced down enemies and survived, of a man who had received orders he didn't like and carried them out anyway because that was his job, of a man who hid his own feelings and carried on.

It was not a face he had shown Sam Beckett very often.

"Things at the Project," he said, enunciating each word carefully, "are just fine. Everything is going as expected."

Baffled, Sam stared back. "Then why are you acting this way? Al, we're friends. What's going on? Is it Tina?"

Al flinched.

"It *is* Tina, isn't it?"

"No," the Observer said, his gravelly voice hoarser now. "It isn't Tina. It's Janna. My—wife."

Wife. Wife?

"You're not married," Sam said, barely hearing his own words. "You used to be. Did you get married again, after—after I left?"

"I guess I did." Al looked weary again. "I wasn't married the last time I walked into the Imaging Chamber, but when I left it, I was."

Something in Sam Beckett's forebrain kicked into high gear, ducking around holes in his memory, examining the ramifications of the Observer's statement. It took a few minutes, staring past Al's head, to reach a conclusion.

"Why didn't we think of that before?" he whispered.

"What do you mean? You did think of it," Al snapped, remembering years of minor changes, years of asking Ziggy every time he prepared to leave the Imaging Chamber. "I don't know what it is you do, but sometimes Tina and Gooshie are married and sometimes they aren't, sometimes *you're*"—Al abruptly changed gears—"sometimes Verbeena has a doctorate in psychology and sometimes in psychiatry, sometimes—this is the part that really drives me nuts—we're overrun seven million bucks and sometimes we're on budget. And up until now I've been five times divorced and still single, but this time I'm married.

"And unless there's somebody else running around mucking up the past, Sam, it's all your fault. We've got to get you home, just to make things settle down!"

"But if . . . if things change every time you leave the Imaging Chamber, when you go back you'll probably be single again, right? So everything should be okay again?"

The impassive face was gone, replaced by another Sam had seen only once before—when he'd told the Observer he wouldn't change the past to save Al's first marriage, the one to Beth. It was a look of such anguish he closed his eyes against it, and heard Al's next words that much more clearly.

"When I go back," Al agreed, speaking very softly, "I'll probably be single again. Janna will be somebody I never met, or somebody I only know from work. And I don't want that, Sam. I don't want this to change. I love her."

"But to stay married to her . . . ," Sam whispered, already knowing the answer, unable to finish the sentence.

Al finished it for him, mercilessly. "To stay married to her, I can't risk going back."

CHAPTER
SEVENTEEN

Kevin Hodge slid out from under his truck and wiped grease off his hands. Bethica was standing over him, tapping her foot impatiently.

"So?" he said. "What?"

"Are you still having that party tonight?"

"Yeah, sure. Why not?"

"Are you going to have beer and booze?"

Kevin got to his feet and looked down at her. "Of course we're going to have beer and booze. It isn't a party otherwise."

"Good," she said, and turned and stomped off.

"Unless Wickie takes it away from you again," one of his friends mocked. "Wickie's good at taking stuff away from you."

Bethica stopped and turned around.

Kevin glared at the boys. "Not any more."

His friends laughed at him. "You shoulda seen your face," one unwary kid sitting on the tailgate of the truck said.

In two strides Kevin crossed to the back of the truck, reached up and took the boy by the neck, hauled him out of the truck bed and threw him on the ground. "You got something to say?"

The boy remained where he was, stunned.

Bethica backed away several steps and watched him warily. Kevin wheeled around to glare at her, too. "What are you looking at?"

"Nothing," she assured him. "Nothing, Kevin."

He was staring at her with a kind of madness blazing in his eyes. "He's not going to make a fool of me twice," he said in a voice so low only she could hear. "Nobody makes a fool of me, not like that. You hear me, Beth? I'll kill him if he tries. And you know I mean it."

Then, raising his voice, he said, "I'm getting a whole keg this time, and I'm picking it up myself. So don't anybody worry. There's going to be lots of booze up on the mountain this time, lots of food. It's going to be the best party all year."

The other boys looked at each other meaningfully. They'd all heard that before. When Kevin spun around to look at them again, they chorused assent. Bethica had heard it too, and she too knew better than to challenge him. There was more going on here than just a quarter-keg of beer or a wrestling match in a parking lot.

She also knew when it was a good idea to get away from Kevin, and she hurried away while he was still basking in the approval of his peers. She was still angry, at herself, at Kevin, at Wickie. So Wickie thought he could lecture to her like she was some little kid? Well, she *wasn't* a little kid, and Wickie ought to know it. The party would go on as planned. Now all she had to do was find something great to wear. And hope Wickie didn't do anything more to tick Kevin off.

"I can't do that stuff," Wickie muttered.

"Why not?" Verbeena asked reasonably. "It's not so hard."

Wickie snorted to himself. "You're a doctor. You're smart."

Verbeena wondered what he'd say if he realized whose body he was in—a man who'd been on the cover of *Time*, genius, Man of the Year. One of the smartest men of all time.

Wickie might not exactly be in Sam Beckett's league, but he was no dummy, either. Someone somewhere along the line had tried to give him a start. Despite his insecurity, he was making a decent try at the problems in the text he'd asked for, and he asked good questions, and he was more interested in the phenomenon of Leaping than frightened by it. In order to explain what little she understood of the physics, she'd had to start over with basic math. What he really wanted to do was talk to Ziggy, but there had to be limits. She didn't know how much memory he'd retain of his visit to the future.

But he was an eager student, and Verbeena loved to teach. She gathered her dashiki around her and sat cross-legged on the floor of the Waiting Room and indulged them both, joyfully.

"Al, I'm sorry," Sam whispered. "I don't know what to say."

Al shrugged, sliding his feelings behind a shield. "I don't know what to say either. We went up to Santa Fe, had lunch, did some shopping. Not much to fall in love on, is it?"

Sam bit his lip. "I guess it's enough." He didn't comment on the things Al had left out. "You don't know for sure that things will be different when you go back," he offered.

"Shall I have Ziggy figure the odds?" Bitterness filled the Observer's voice for a moment, then disappeared, to be replaced by resignation. "It doesn't make much difference, does it? It doesn't do me a lot of good being married to her if I have to spend all my time with you to keep it that way. I lost her the minute I stepped back into the Imaging Chamber."

"She's not *gone*, Al. She didn't cease to exist because of something I've done. She's alive somewhere now, doing something that probably leads her to the Project. Do you

159

remember her from—from before the last time?"

Al shrugged. "I think I do. She was just somebody around, not a direct report. How was I supposed to know? I was with Tina!"

"What about Tina now?"

"Tina's happily married to Gooshie, has been for six months."

"But Gooshie has bad breath," Sam protested.

"I know," Al said, expelling a cloud of cigar smoke.

The two of them looked at each other, mystified.

"You know, it's not just your life—that suddenly you're married when you weren't before. Janna's life changed too. But since she's not here—she must be connected somehow to somebody I've met here," Sam said thoughtfully, as they changed the subject by mutual agreement. "It's a ripple effect. I'm the stone in the pond, and your life and Janna's are somewhere out of my sight, but you've been hit by the ripple changes from this Leap. You could ask Ziggy about that."

Al raised an eyebrow and tapped the handlink. "Ziggy," he said, speaking now to the computer controlling the Imaging Chamber in which his physical body remained, "how's Janna connected to the people Sam's met in Snow Owl?"

The handlink blinked, pink, yellow, blue cubes glowing in sequence, slowly, then more rapidly. Al tapped in a code pattern. The light sequence repeated.

"Ziggy can't find a connection," Al announced. "Who knows, Sam. Even if we did find out, it wouldn't make any difference. Things would still change. They'll keep changing until we find a way to get you home for good."

Home for good.

Sam closed his eyes against a sudden unbearable rush of homesickness. He could only remember glimpses of the Project, of his family, of his own past. He could barely remember any more what his own face looked like. He'd been Leaping so long. . . .

"I'd go home if I knew how, Al," he said quietly.

"I know, Sam." Al reached out in a futile effort to touch Sam's shoulder, a touch that couldn't connect, could offer no comfort.

Sam drew a long shuddering breath. "Okay," he said, straightening up again. "Things will keep on changing. They'll always affect you and the Project, to a greater or lesser extent. We don't know how to keep that from happening; in fact, as long as the purpose of my Leaping is to change things, we *can't* prevent it from happening. That's a strict parameter. So we have to live with it until . . . we can stop making changes. Right?"

"Right." Al tapped at his cigar. The ash fell and disappeared.

"That means you have to go back and find out the most efficient change I can make that will let me Leap. And you have to go back, too, to work with Ziggy and, and . . ."

"And Gooshie and Tina and Verbeena," Al supplied quickly, so the failure of memory wouldn't be quite so obvious.

"Gooshie and Tina and Verbeena," Sam said, as if reading them back into his memory. He knew the names. He wasn't quite sure what role each of them had at the Project. In any case it seemed that the roles involved were in flux. "And look for some way to find out what went wrong."

And bring me home again.

He didn't say it. He didn't have to.

"So I go back." Al's voice was expressionless.

Sam looked at him carefully, aware of the weight and measure of his words, of what he was asking, aware that he had to ask it anyway. "Al, this sounds selfish, I know, but once I'm home, you might still be married to her. Or if you aren't, you could marry her then."

"It won't be the same," Al grumbled softly. It did sound as if this plan were wholly to Sam's benefit, but on the other hand . . . there was no other hand. He couldn't spend the rest of his life in the Imaging Chamber, watching Sam; even if he did, he still wouldn't be with Janna.

"Ziggy does say you need to find a way to keep Bethica from going to that party, but since that's when she talks Kevin out of killing Wickie, there's a sort of conflict of interest going on."

"Does Ziggy have any suggestions?"

"Not yet," Al said, studying the handlink.

"Then maybe you ought to go help Ziggy find out what the connection is between Janna and this Leap," Sam said softly.

Al met his eyes, his fingers poised over the handlink to send the code that would open the Door and end his relationship. He said nothing. His fingers touched the link. The Door opened, Al nodded once, sharply, and stepped through. The Door closed behind him.

"Good luck," Sam whispered.

No one else came into the bar that afternoon. Sam finished cleaning up, mopped down the floor, dusted everything in sight. He'd expected Kevin, or someone fronting for Kevin, to come in and buy another keg, but no one came. He was spending more time alone on this Leap than he could remember in a long time.

He half wished Davey would come in so he could try again to teach him to play "Chopsticks," even though he knew it would be a futile effort. He wondered if the boy compared himself to other people and felt bad about his own limitations, his irrational rages. They weren't remotely his fault, but no one would ever be able to explain that to him. Eighteen or nineteen years ago, fetal alcohol syndrome wasn't that well known anyway. He wondered when Rimae had found out that her adopted son was irreversibly retarded, and found himself flinching with sympathy at her reaction. Grief. Anger. And an overwhelming urge to protect her son, forever.

He had just closed down for the afternoon break when the telephone rang. He picked it up uncertainly.

"Polar Bar."

It was Rimae. "Are you planning on picking up your paycheck or what? You better get on over here."

A sudden vision of his first glimpse of Rimae flashed into his mind, and he said warily, "I could pick it up when I come in to work this evening, if you don't mind. I've got some things I want to take care of."

There was a long amazed silence at the other end of the line. "Are you feeling okay?"

"Oh, sure. I'm fine. I've just got, you know, errands to run."

Rimae didn't sound pleased. "You know what you're missing, don't you?"

Sam swallowed, dry throated. "Yes. But I'll take a rain check, if you don't mind." He winced as he said it.

Rimae laughed. "Need to get some raincoats?"

Sam winced again. He didn't like puns, unless he was the one making them. On purpose.

Rimae didn't wait for an answer. "Well, we're booked for a private party at eight—a bachelorette party for Suzie McAllister. So you'd probably need all your strength up anyway. I'll bring the check. And stand by to protect you, if you like."

Sam almost said, "Who's going to protect me from you?" but considering the tales he'd heard about bachelorette parties, he reconsidered. "Okay," he responded. "I'll see you then."

Hanging up the phone, he wondered if Al would be back in time. It was the kind of situation the Observer normally rejoiced in, watching his strait-laced friend writhing under the attentions of several dozen slightly looped females with sex on their minds. Al still might, he thought, even if he was happily married. Still happily married, that is.

It wasn't selfish to want to go home, he reminded himself. It was the best thing for everyone. Al agreed. Everyone agreed.

Except, of course, for God, or time, or whatever had him Leaping to begin with.

CHAPTER
EIGHTEEN

Al stood still in the middle of the Imaging Chamber, not moving. His omnipresent cigar had burned out somehow. The walls of the Chamber were blank, white, empty. He could hear a high-pitched hum of power pouring through the walls, the ceiling, the floor—it was the Accelerator powering down, Ziggy returning the centering function to a rest-and-ready state. He was standing on a silver disk, beneath another silver disk; the two disks and his own attire, a dark red suit with a dark blue tie, provided the only color in the room. Even the handlink had gone blank in his hand.

Usually, at this point, he was asking Ziggy questions about some crisis Sam had gotten himself into, or at the very least asking about the status of the Project. He didn't feel like asking this time. He'd have to eventually, he knew that, but for the time being he didn't want to say anything. He didn't want to go anywhere. He didn't want to move.

He was remembering his wedding day, as if fixing those details firmly in his mind would make them real.

He remembered wrapping a napkin around a champagne glass—no, that was Ruthie. He remembered an arch of swords; no, that was his very first wedding, his first love, Beth. Then a judge's chambers, where he had made a jaunty salute to a ruling that Beth's new marriage would stand. Sam hadn't let him change that history, didn't help him prevent Beth from marrying someone else. Wouldn't tell her Al was still alive, a POW in Vietnam. So Al married again. And again.

It was past history now. All past history, though he could remember that anguish still. He loved Beth to this day, more than any of his subsequent wives. He could still see her soft brown eyes filled with tears as she danced that last dance, never knowing she was dancing with her lost love who was giving her up of his own free will.

As he'd be giving up Janna when he walked through that door, whether they were still married in this version of the present or not.

The moments stretched out. He looked down at the cigar, rolling it back and forth between his fingers, the brown leaves crinkling under the pressure. All he had to do was ask Ziggy, and Ziggy would tell him. It would be simple, quick, and reliable, and he'd pass through the Accelerator airlock knowing exactly what he'd be walking into.

He drew a deep breath and let it go, shivering a little. The Imaging Chamber was cold. It had to be; the Project required massive amounts of power, and Ziggy's components were even more vulnerable to heat than most computers. Ziggy was silent.

He took one more glance around, as if fixing the empty room in his memory, and stepped off the disk toward the airlock door. It purred open before him, slid shut again, and the other door of the airlock opened in its turn. He was standing at the top of the ramp down to the Control Room, and he paused, scanning, to see who was waiting.

No one. A pair of white-suited lab techs, working on circuitry normally hidden by the panel propped up against the wall beside them. No anxious congressmen wanting to know about budget, no security people, no Verbeena with news of something having gone wrong with the Visitor. No Janna, waiting to welcome him back. No one.

Perfectly normal, in other words.

He drew a deep breath, discarded the cigar butt in the receptacle provided at the top of the ramp (when did that get put there? he wondered), and started down and across the room toward the Waiting Room. He couldn't help it. He had to meet the Visitor. It was long past time.

Wickie was by himself, doing a steady series of abdominal crunches eerily reminiscent of Sam's, a few days—and thirty-some years—before. There wasn't even anyone up in the Observation Deck. Al's eyes narrowed. Someone was going to hear about deserting their station that way.

"About time somebody showed up," the Visitor said, sitting up and wiping the sheen of sweat off his face with the towel hanging off the end of the bed. "They expect me to spend all my time reading books around here?"

"How long since someone was here?" Al asked, going over to a chair, turning it around and sitting in it backward.

Wickie leaned back in his own chair, one foot on the edge of the table, balancing on the two rear legs. "Dunno. Few hours maybe. I'm telling you, I'm getting awfully pissed off at being locked up so long. You keep telling me I'm not a prisoner, but you won't let me go anywhere." The other man studied Al thoughtfully. "If it weren't for what I see in the mirror, I'd think I was in jail."

Al nodded. "I can see how you'd think that way. But it's like you were told—if you're not here at the right time, you might never get back at all. We're not sure. So we don't want to take any chances."

"I think I'll go on buying that for about a day or two more," Wickie said evenly. "Then I think I'll go for a little walk."

Al hid a grim smile. He had no doubt that Wickie would attempt to break out as promised, or that he might even get as far as the Control Room. But they'd beefed up their security after a few such scares—one in particular, when Leon Stryker, a serial killer Sam had Leaped into, actually got all the way out of the Project, stole a vehicle, made it into the nearest town—and he wasn't particularly nervous about Wickie getting away from them. Besides, the Visitor wasn't being belligerent about it. He had a good argument; it just wasn't a risk the Project chose to take.

"Treating you okay otherwise?"

Wickie shrugged, the muscles of his shoulders—Sam's shoulders—sliding under the brown T-shirt. "I could use a little companionship, if you know what I mean."

"Sorry."

Wickie smiled, an echo of Sam Beckett's own rare, infectious grin. "Didn't think you'd go for it."

"Got a question for you," Al said after a moment. He wished he could smoke here; he wanted a cigar in the worst way right now. He wasn't carrying any with him, either.

"Shoot." Wickie rocked back and forth.

"Do you know anybody named Janna?" What was her maiden name? For one panicked moment Al couldn't remember. "Janna Fulkes." That was it. Fulkes.

For a moment Al had been afraid he couldn't recall his wife's maiden name because she wasn't his wife in this moment. But he knew it, and his memories of her were still solid. He'd have to ask Ziggy to be sure, but—

"Never heard of her," Wickie said flatly. "Who is she?"

"Are you sure? Maybe before you moved to Snow Owl?"

The hazel-green eyes were amused. Wickie reached up to brush a stray lock of hair, brown with an incongruous white streak, out of his eyes. Sam needed a haircut. "Sure I'm sure. What about her?"

Al shook his head. "I was hoping you knew her."

"I could tell. Who is she?"

"My wife."

After a startled pause, Wickie burst out laughing, rocking forward to set all four legs of his chair on the floor. "That's the first time any man ever told me he was sorry I *didn't* know his wife!"

Unwilling, Al had to laugh too. He'd been in that position a few times himself. "Get around a lot, do you?"

168

Wickie shook his head, still chuckling. "I get my share," he said. "I don't have to worry about cold nights much."

Remembering Rimae, Al was willing to bet on it. Wickie didn't seem disposed to name names or expound on his conquests, though, which upped him a notch in Al's esteem. While he wouldn't mind comparing notes over a few beers, still, he had to give the guy credit for discretion.

As for Janna, well, it didn't exactly solve the problem, but it narrowed it down a little. Janna must be linked to someone else in Snow Owl. Which meant he'd have to have a long talk with Ziggy.

He stood up, twirling the chair back into place. "Anything I can get you? Other than 'companionship,' that is?"

"Crossword puzzle, maybe?"

Al had learned long ago not to be surprised at Visitors. "Sure, we can get you crossword puzzles. As many as you want." He was glad Wickie hadn't asked *why* Al wanted to know; it would be just one more thing the Visitor would have to forget when he returned to his own time and self.

He left quickly, aware of the Visitor watching him as the door slid away for him and back again, shutting Wickie away from the rest of the Project. His path took him back through the Control Room again, past it and into the administrative office corridor, past Sam's "upper-level" office and back to his own again.

He scanned it quickly. Nothing was different, as far as he could tell. The same plaques and citations on the walls, the same gleaming desktop, the same stack of papers in the In and Out baskets.

Well, maybe the In basket was a little closer to overflowing than the last time he'd been in here, but that was to be expected.

He pulled the office door shut and sat down at the desk. "Ziggy?" he said to the ceiling.

"About time," the computer replied promptly, annoyance in its voice. "I thought you were going to ignore me completely."

"Like I could," Al muttered sarcastically. "Give me a status report, please."

"Unchanged."

The wave of relief that swept over him was almost too intense to bear. "Thank you," he whispered.

"You're welcome," Ziggy answered.

"I wasn't talking to you."

"Well! You don't have to be rude."

This, coming from Ziggy, was almost enough to make Al laugh again.

"Glad you're amused," the computer remarked acidly.

Al shook his head, still smiling. "Okay, Ziggy. It's just . . . nervous reaction.

"We need to know how Janna's tied in to this Leap."

"Why don't you ask her?"

Al opened his mouth to make a cutting response, and closed it again, slowly. Finally he said, "I'd have to tell her why."

"I could summarize it for you."

"No. No, I don't want to ask her, and I don't want to explain." He could see himself explaining to her, *I'm only temporarily married to you, honey, we've got to enjoy this while we can* . . . . Come to think of it, he could have used that line in several of his marriages, if he'd only known.

"Just do the data search, okay? And don't ask Janna anything. I don't want her to know."

Some hours later, Al looked around the bedroom, checking the details against the new memories. Same woven cotton bedspread, same maple rocking chair on a rag rug in the corner, same pillowcases with a green foil-wrapped mint set squarely in the center of each one. Mints on the pillow. It was a private joke between them. It always made him smile. She'd never admit she put them there; must be some genie from a brass lamp who came up with them, she always said.

Folded neatly at the bottom of the bed was an old-fashioned quilt. Janna liked the country look. It was utterly alien to Al, who'd spent most of his life in the Navy and the rest of it roaming, but comforting somehow. It was Janna, and that made it home.

"Ziggy?" he said quietly.

The computer, triggered by the sound of its name, responded, "Monitoring, Admiral."

"Search for a link between"—he swallowed, unable to believe for a moment in any past, much less one as stable as this appeared to be—"between Janna and all the people Sam's dealing with on the current Leap. Trace the events that led to—" he took a deep breath—"this."

"Acknowledging, Admiral."

He heard the door slide open, heard her footsteps. "Don't monitor these quarters. Send a summary to the terminal in my office under secure lock."

"Yes, Admiral." He could hear the "click" that was Ziggy's signal that it had turned its monitors off, and at the same time heard Janna come in from the living room.

He turned to welcome her with open arms. She greeted him with a smile and a kiss, stepping into his arms as if she always did that, as if she belonged there.

"Hello, baby," he whispered into her hair. "Missed you."

"Well, I missed you too," she said, nuzzling him back, "but I didn't think you'd been gone that long. Al, you're breaking my ribs! Is everything okay?"

"So far." He could have bitten his tongue off. He didn't want to interrupt the moment. Reluctantly, he loosened his embrace.

"Al?" She pulled away, looking him in the eye. "What is it?"

"It's nothing. Nothing."

"Albert Calavicci, don't you try to lie to me. Something's wrong, isn't it? Is it Sam? Has something happened?"

"No. Nothing's happened to Sam. He's fine. He's got to keep a kid from going to a party, that's all, and then he'll Leap again."

171

But he couldn't meet her eyes, even when she took his face between her hands and gently held it, mere inches from her own. "Then why are you so knotted up inside, honey?"

He tried to smile and couldn't. "I'm sorry, sweetheart, I can't talk about it. I *can't.*"

He couldn't. He couldn't make himself talk to her. If he asked her, and she answered, he'd have to go back and tell Sam—and run the risk of not finding her there when he came back.

Instead his hands slid down her sides and he took her in his arms again and held her as if he would never, never, never let her go.

Recognizing a losing battle when she fought one, Janna sighed and cooperated with the inevitable. "Al?" she whispered in his ear.

"Mmm-hmmm?" he responded absentmindedly, wishing women's fashions still featured buttons or zippers or something a man could make sense of.

"Does this mean I get to go shopping again?"

"Later," he muttered.

She giggled and nipped at his ear. "I know this lovely little gallery on Water Street—"

Now it was his turn to pull away. "Are you nuts?" he said, with mock indignation. "Are you trying to send me to the poorhouse?"

She laughed at him, and he laughed back, and shut away the voice in the back of his mind that echoed, " . . . *you have to go back and find out the most efficient change I can make that will let me Leap. . . .*"

It was the weight and measure of friendship, against the weight and measure of love, and Al closed his eyes and set aside the scales one more time.

CHAPTER
NINETEEN

Verbeena generally avoided eating with Tina; the Project's chief computer architect didn't have a lot of interesting conversation. She was always either wrapped up in some esoteric computer journal or engrossed in a debate on the merits of various shades of nail polish. Verbeena couldn't decide whether Tina was too smart for her, too dumb, or both.

Today, however, she invited herself to a place at Tina's table in the cafeteria for dinner. Tina looked up at her in some surprise. She wore, as most of the other Project personnel did, a white lab coat. Unlike most of the other Project personnel, Tina wore her coat this evening over a short body-clinging electric blue satin dress with a short frilly skirt and matching blue hose.

Verbeena's preferred leisure attire leaned more to flowing caftans. She supposed she was in no position to criticize.

"Dr. Beeks!" Tina chirped. "How nice of you to stop by. Are you having the chicken? I think the chicken is just, you know, terrific. . . ."

Verbeena smiled and unfolded a napkin into her lap. "Terrific" was too strong a word, in her opinion. Chicken and broccoli, in what purported to be lemon sauce, would never be her first choice anyway. Some days she thought she'd kill for a good jambalaya. Tina was eating what looked like corn clam chowder. With the right spices, Verbeena thought, that might almost work.

"How's it going, Dr. Martinez-O'Farrell?" she said politely in return.

Tina looked bewildered. "Are you mad at me, Dr. Beeks?"

"Of course not. Why ever would you think so?"

"Nobody around here calls me Dr. Martinez-O'Farrell unless they're being, like, really really formal, or they're mad at me or something." Tina batted huge blue eyes. Verbeena resisted the impulse to check to see if the napkin had survived the resulting breeze.

"Well, hardly anyone calls me Dr. Beeks, either," she pointed out reasonably, sawing at the chicken. She managed to tear a piece loose and put it in her mouth, chewing determinedly. "Except Gooshie. And you."

"But you're a *doctor* Doctor."

This almost made sense. Verbeena considered it, managed to swallow the bite of chicken, and smiled. "Tell you what. You can call me Dr. Beeks when you come in for your physical, okay? Otherwise you can call me Verbeena, and I'll call you Tina. Okay?"

Tina thought about this. "Okay!" she said at last. "We'll be, like, friends!"

"That's right. Like friends."

Tina seemed to run out of things to say to her new friend at that point and, smiling tentatively, bent to her soup. Verbeena was content to let the silence go. There were only half a dozen other people in the cafeteria at this hour, and the two women were separated from the nearest potential listeners by at least fifteen feet.

What on earth could Al Calavicci see in a woman like this when he had Janna, Verbeena wondered. Yet there was no mistaking Al's tightly controlled anguish when he'd told her about the different past on the other side of the Imaging Chamber Door, a past in which Janna was just another face among the hundreds at the Project, and Tina

Martinez-O'Farrell was the object of Al's overwhelming interest. Well, at least that was his version.

The Admiral was known throughout the Project as an outrageous flirt, of course, the kind who left a red rose on every woman's desk at least once a year and would pledge undying love at the drop of an eyelid. In private he'd been known to express a connoisseur's appreciation of the female form. But he was *married,* for heaven's sake, and very happily so. The women at the Project joked about it. If anybody actually took him up on his flirting he'd run like a rabbit.

Which made that other past intriguing. Definitely intriguing. That other Al that *her* Al described was no rabbit. Would be insulted at the very idea, she suspected.

Of course, this Al would be equally insulted. She chuckled to herself.

"I'm sorry?"

Verbeena looked up, startled. She'd been so involved in her thoughts and in the tough chicken that she'd almost forgotten about the other woman at the table.

"Oh, nothing," she said hastily. "I was just thinking about something Al said."

"Al? Admiral Calavicci?" Tina was intent suddenly, and wistful.

Interesting reaction, Verbeena thought. "Mm-hmm. Tell me, Tina, do you remember when you first met Al?"

"Sure I do," she said promptly. "The first night I got here. There was a party." She smiled a little. "It was right here. Dr. Beckett played the piano—that piano over there— and Al and I danced." She twirled her spoon in her soup, moving pieces of clam and bits of corn around, and her voice dropped. "There were a lot of new people there that night. Janna was there, too. Jessie Olivera—you know, from the Senate liaison office?—she says Al and Janna fell in love that night. Love at first sight.

"Do you believe in love at first sight, Verbeena?"

The high-pitched, Marilyn Monroe breathiness was missing from her voice now. She sounded thoughtful, and sad.

Oh, you poor child, Verbeena thought in a rush of sympathy. *You're plain crazy about the man, aren't you?*

"I think two people can be attracted to each other the first time they see each other," she said. "They say it's pheromones. That sort of takes the magic out of it, though."

Tina smiled again, wry. "But that's not really love."

"Honey, I don't know for sure what love is, and nobody else can tell you either. Sometimes that attraction just disappears, poof like magic, and nobody knows why. One minute two people are crazy for each other, and the next they're not."

"Sometimes people stay in love for years."

"Sometimes," Verbeena agreed. "Sometimes only one stays in love and the other one doesn't. That's the really tragic story."

Tina nodded, straightening up. Before Verbeena's eyes she regained her sparkle. "Well, lightning strikes for everybody sometime."

"That's what they say." The Project psychologist smiled too, sadly. The last bite of chicken was as rubbery as the first. It didn't matter any more.

"I think that's got to be the moment," Verbeena said later, to Ziggy and Al. They were in the small conference room next to the administrative offices, a room usually used for meetings of a dozen or fewer. The walls were white, the acoustic tiles in the ceiling were white, the floor was white, the automatic recorder on the wall was white. Verbeena's lab coat was white.

In all that whiteness, the red and black of Al's clothing, the darkness of Verbeena's skin and the deeper darkness of Al's hair and eyes were shocking splashes of color.

"I agree," Ziggy said from the hidden speakers. "But I still haven't been able to determine exactly *why* it happened that way." The computer sounded irritable.

"I don't get it," Al said. He slipped the clear plastic

wrapping—something new, a recycled product Verbeena couldn't remember the name of—off a cigar, crumpling it in one hand as he rolled the cigar back and forth between the fingers of the other. He tossed the wrapper into a nearby wastebasket and trimmed the ends of the cigar with the deft movements of long habit, then gave the edges a thorough examination.

He didn't want to look her in the eyes, Verbeena noted clinically. They were, after all, talking about something very, very personal to a man not accustomed to revealing secrets.

"How do we know this isn't the way it's supposed to be in the first place?" he asked at last, chomping fiercely on the unlit cigar.

"It isn't," Ziggy said flatly. "As you recall, Admiral."

"I'm not sure I do recall that."

Denial, Verbeena thought.

"Dr. Beckett is correct. His actions in the past have affected not only the immediate future of the people around him, but ours—yours—as well. I have initiated a detailed search of the lives of every person with whom Dr. Beckett has been involved on this Leap."

"And what have you discovered, Ziggy?"

"Unfortunately, as yet, nothing."

It was no wonder the computer sounded irritable. Ziggy was linked to both Sam and Al; at times it was almost like talking to one or the other of them. When Ziggy was irritated, it sounded exactly like a female version of Al. Verbeena shuddered at the thought.

"If there isn't anything to tell him, there's no reason to renew contact," Al said, still examining the cigar.

Verbeena folded her hands in her lap and simply looked at him.

"Perhaps," she said finally, keeping her voice as neutral as possible, "you could try going from the other direction, Ziggy."

"Please clarify your suggestion, Dr. Beeks."

"Instead of looking at it from the perspective of the people surrounding Sam, how about looking at it from Janna's point of view? Wouldn't it be easier to trace back the records of one person's life than trying to trace forward the possibilities for several people?"

There was a pause. Verbeena thought she could feel the subliminal humming of the air circulation, of the electricity powering Ziggy pouring through the wires in the walls. She could hear the whisper of the cigar rolling back and forth between Al's fingertips. She suppressed the urge to snatch the cylinder out of his hands, to crumble it onto the floor and stomp on it. She could not stand the smell of those cigars. Government regulations said there would be no smoking anywhere inside Project buildings; they'd decided long since to turn a blind eye to smoking inside private personnel quarters, and Verbeena was morally certain Al lit up as soon as he walked into the Imaging Chamber. There was a reason for that ashtray at the top of the ramp, after all. Elsewhere in the Project—in rooms like this one—Al chewed on unlit stogies.

Of course, he hated it when she called them "stogies."

"It's a sound suggestion." Ziggy sounded annoyed, probably because the idea hadn't come from it to begin with.

"I guess so," Al said. There was a thread of resignation in his voice. He drew in a deep breath, almost a shudder, and looked up at last. "Nothing lasts forever, after all."

He meant his marriage, Verbeena realized. He was saying goodbye to it, cutting himself off from it.

"Al, we don't know how things will work out on this end." She was trying to be reassuring.

He wasn't accepting it. He didn't want reassurance or empty comfort. He was looking at an ending with open eyes and cold knowledge, and he didn't need help with it.

"You first met Janna at your birthday party, back in '93, didn't you?" Verbeena asked. If he wanted to deal with reality, well, that was one of the things she was good at.

"There were a lot of new people there. Tina was one of them, wasn't she?"

The heavy dark eyebrows knit in confusion. "Yes, I—I remember that." His eyes squeezed shut, as if his vision had blurred momentarily and he were seeing double. "I met Tina that night, too." He shook his head sharply. "This is a bizarre feeling. I can't keep things straight."

Verbeena sat up a little straighter. "Can you remember *not* falling in love with Janna that night?"

He rubbed the bridge of his nose. "I can remember—Sam was working in his lab, and I called down and told him to come on up and join the party." He spoke with assurance. His next words were slower, more uncertain. "I met . . . a lot of people that night. I met Janna—no, she wasn't there, or—was she?" The look in his eyes was a little frantic. "Verbeena, how am I supposed to remember something that didn't happen?"

"But it *did* happen," Verbeena said. "You told me so."

For a moment she wondered if they weren't both crazy. Al was right; how could he remember something that never happened? If a patient of hers said that, she'd say he was delusional. *Was* Al delusional? Was the whole Project a figment of someone's fevered imagination?

If it weren't for the EEG tracings and the responses of the man in the Waiting Room, she'd commit Al in a minute. Lock him up in a rubber room, as they used to joke in the darker moments of her residency.

And put herself in the next room over.

But the man in the Waiting Room was a man named Wickie Gray Wolf Starczynski, in the body of Sam Beckett.

And Wickie swore that it was June 1975. The president was Gerald Ford. He was vaguely aware of Snow Owl's plans for the Bicentennial. And he didn't know about anything after that.

All past—any past—experience indicated that Sam had to fix something that had gone wrong—in the past.

She was sick and tired of recapitulating.

"Janna Fulkes arrived at the Project in one timeline on June fifteenth, 1993, your birthday. In another she joined us five days later." Ziggy recited as if the computer were a little girl standing up in front of her third-grade class, doing a book report.

"Five days later?" Al and Verbeena chorused, staring at each other. "How do you know?" Verbeena went on. "If that isn't a real past any more, how can you know?"

"I told you, Dr. Beeks," and suddenly the little girl's voice was very sad, "I don't participate. I observe."

"So because she was five days late, I didn't fall in love with her?" Al said mutinously.

"By that time you were thoroughly involved with Tina Martinez-O'Farrell."

"In only five days?"

"Al," Verbeena reminded him, "you've fallen in love in less time, with less excuse, several times before." Before you were married, she thought but did not say.

"That's not the same thing!" Al slid from mutiny to indignation without missing a beat.

"It's never the same thing," Verbeena said dryly. "Ziggy, why was Janna late in that other past?"

The little girl's voice was gone, replaced by an adult woman's. "I don't know that yet, Dr. Beeks."

Verbeena opened her mouth to ask why and then reconsidered. She did *not* want to get into another metaphysical discussion of spacetime and Ziggy's place in it, or out of it, or wherever it was.

"Well, let us know," she said briskly. "Meanwhile, don't you need to get back there, Al, and give Sam the new pieces to our little puzzle?"

"We appear to be losing sight of the essential problem," Ziggy reminded them.

"What do you mean?" Al snapped, still not comfortable with the idea of going back. "I think I've got it pretty clearly in mind."

"The essential problem is still to discover what it is that

Dr. Beckett has to put right. You've forgotten, Admiral, that what led to this present is what has gone wrong."

"That can't be right," Verbeena objected. "Unless the past is slipping and sliding all over the place without Sam's help."

"What do you mean?" Al asked, confused.

"The past that used to be, before Sam arrived to change it, led to your involvement with Tina. Right?"

"Right," Al and Ziggy chorused, in exactly the same wary tone.

"Then Sam arrived and started changing things. As a result, Janna got here on time, you met her, fell in love, and here we are. Right? So maybe the wrong Sam's supposed to be putting right is that you didn't get together with Janna in the first place!"

"Then why hasn't Sam Leaped?" Al said bluntly.

"It's far more likely—an eighty-seven-percent probability—that some change he has made in his effort to save Bethica caused this situation to begin with," Ziggy agreed. "It may even be that he remains in Snow Owl to correct the details. In this case, one of the results would be to put things back the way they were for the Admiral."

"Whether I want him to or not," Al muttered under his breath. "Sometimes all this damned do-gooding really gets on my nerves."

"Or," Ziggy continued, "there's a ninety-percent chance that the whole business with the Admiral and Janna Fulkes has nothing to do with Dr. Beckett's task in this Leap at all, and the whole situation is nothing more than an unfortunate side effect."

"Oh." Verbeena hadn't thought it through that far. "Oh, dear. I'm sorry, Al, I really am."

Al let go a deep breath. "You know the only good part about this, Verbeena?"

"Is there a good part?" she muttered, and then caught herself. Never act despondent around a patient: first rule of client counseling. "What?"

"Once the past changes, you won't remember any of this. It'll never have happened, from your point of view. And Janna won't remember either."

"But you will, won't you?" she said softly.

Al's eyes were bleak. "I'm linked to Ziggy, and to Sam, with his photographic memory. I won't forget Janna, any more than I could ever forget Beth.

"I can't. And"—he paused, and the look on his face made her want to cry—"I think, this time, I want to."

CHAPTER

TWENTY

Al was dressed in silver and shades of blue, from his silver shoes to his dark royal blue shirt. He walked up the ramp, through the airlock doors of the Accelerator, into the Imaging Chamber.

Sometimes, on walking into this room, he remembered the frisson of fear he'd experienced the first time he'd entered it. He had no idea, back then, whether whatever it was that happened to Sam would happen to him too.

God or Fate or Chance, Time or Whatever, he had long since decided, didn't want him to get any closer to Leaping than he already had. If he'd given it more thought he would have concluded that Whatever had run him through the wringer often enough, thank you. His job on this adventure was to be the Observer, to coach, to supply information, to provide moral support. Not to burden the Leaper with his personal problems, any more than a good commanding officer burdened his troops. He'd already said too much to Sam. It was time to go back to business as usual.

The room was plain white, with panels set in the walls, a disk in the middle of the floor and a matching disk hanging in the air overhead. The lighting gave the room a blue cast, made it feel cold. Al paused to light his cigar, a personal gesture of self-fortification, and, pressing the power switch on the handlink, he stepped onto the floor disk. "Ziggy. Center me on Sam."

Around him, the room began to blur and spin, and he shut his eyes briefly. The sound of a Door opening was his signal. He looked up to see Sam, standing behind a bar, against which a dozen women crowded.

They were laughing, teasing, munching peanuts and bar mix. Sam was looking frazzled and frantic.

Sam never did know how to appreciate a golden opportunity, Al thought. He stepped "forward"—some part of him knew he was still in the Imaging Chamber, still standing on the disk, but he'd long ago stopped worrying about that—walked through the bar, and leaned over Sam's shoulder.

"Too much vermouth in that gin," he advised.

Sam shared a sickly grin between Al and the middle-aged, overweight woman who'd ordered the martini with double onions just as she added, "I think those two little balls are just *so* cute."

Al did a double take. "Uh-oh. Sam, when women turn into party animals, things can get out of control."

"I know," Sam muttered frantically. The overweight woman was yelping with laughter.

"I want a screwdriver," another woman announced. "C'mon, Wickie, make me a screwdriver."

"Um, uh, sure."

The level of uncertainty in Sam's voice pulled Al's attention away, at least temporarily, from the buxom brunette's cleavage. "You *do* know how to make a screwdriver, don't you?" he asked.

"Of course," Sam snapped, reaching for a bottle of vodka.

Al grinned. "Of course, it can be a lot of fun when they go out of control, too. . . ."

"I think I'll have a Handyman's Special," someone else said. "I hear you're really handy, Wickie!"

"We know why you're the bartender, honey. You want to keep that bar between you and us!"

"Aw, look, he's blushing! I never knew Indians could blush!"

Sam muttered something about ignorance under his breath. One of the women at the bar said, "What was that, Wickie love?"

"It was the Indian Love Call," someone else cracked.

Sam bit his lower lip. Al could see him about to snap at the woman; instead he said politely, "You ladies will have to excuse me a minute," and headed for the men's room, followed by catcalls and offers of help.

Al followed him in, to find Sam leaning back against a sink, staring at the ceiling. Al looked around. The men's room at the Polar Bar was considerably cleaner than many of its kind.

"Classy place," he remarked.

"Yeah, it's a shame the clientele isn't classy too. Do you have anything?"

Brought back to reality, or at least to the here and now, Al looked at the handlink. The light patterns translated themselves into information; how, he wasn't sure. That was the techie stuff. It was Sam's department. All Al cared about was whether it worked.

He didn't much want to answer the question, either. "Er, no. We're working on another angle. What's the party here for?"

"It's a bachelorette party," Sam said grimly.

Now that was the sort of distraction a man could do something with. Al chortled. "Are you going to be jumping out of a cake later in the evening?"

If looks could kill, Al would have been dead several Leaps ago; he'd developed ignoring Sam's glares into a fine art.

"No, I am not jumping out of a cake." Each word was spaced out. Seeing the Observer's incorrigible grin, he gave up and returned to the most pressing issue. "If I'm supposed to keep Bethica from being crippled in a car wreck, though, I think I've figured out how to do it."

Al arched his eyebrows high. "Hey, I thought *I* was the one with the key to the future." He brandished the handlink

185

in Sam's direction. "What, are you trying to do me out of a job here?"

"Kevin's having a party later night, and he's coming by to pick up the liquor. And I'm not going to give it to him. Case closed."

"Except, of course . . ." Al prodded.

"Except I haven't Leaped," Sam admitted. "Something's going to go wrong, isn't it?"

"Naturally." Al took a deep drag on his cigar and exhaled a thunderhead of blue smoke. "I dunno what yet, but something. There's always the little detail that Bethica *has* to go to talk him out of trying to kill you."

Sam studied him quizzically. "You're more cheerful than you were the last time," he remarked. "I don't know why that doesn't seem particularly comforting." He'd straightened up, crossing his arms over his chest. "I don't think Kevin would really do it, anyway. He's just a kid."

Al punched keys on the handlink. "But he's a *mean* kid, Sam. Ziggy says not only does Bethica still go up there, but . . . what?" He slapped the recalcitrant piece of hardware. "Okay. There's still a sixty-seven-percent chance Bethica's going to end up in a wheelchair, and there's a ninety-four-percent chance he runs you off the road."

Sam absorbed this news silently. At last he said, "But Bethica's odds are getting better, aren't they?"

Al looked exasperated. "I know you don't like thinking about yourself," he said with heavy irony, remembering a time or two when Sam, tried beyond his endurance, had attempted to change a Leap for his own benefit, "but could you spare a thought for Wickie? He'd probably like to live, too."

"No matter what I do, somebody's going to get hurt," Sam said without thinking. Then his eyes met Al's, and he drew breath for an apology.

Fists pounded against the bathroom door. "Wickie, sweetie, did you fall in? Do you need help?" The two men

186

could barely distinguish the words in the gales of laughter that accompanied them. Grateful for the distraction, Sam gave Al a desperate look.

"Those women are maniacs," he muttered.

"Yeah, isn't it great?"

"*You'd* think so. I'll bet you *would* jump out of a cake for them."

Al grinned reminiscently. "Don't knock it. I did once. Place called the Tonga Tiki. It was a chocolate-whipped-cream cake, and all the ladies had dessert forks. They were all gathered around, drooling, and I . . ."

"Oh, please. No."

Sam always cut him off before he could get into any of his best stories. He snorted, took another drag on the cigar, and studied the blinking lights of the handlink. They stuttered, and he whacked the handlink with the side of his hand. The pattern steadied, made sense again.

More pounding on the door, with accompanying shouts and hoots and yowls. Sam shuddered. So did Al, but for reasons of his own.

"Ladies, give a man some privacy," Sam shouted at last.

"Wickie, get your tail back out here. You've got thirsty customers." It was Rimae this time, and her order was supported with yips of glee. Then the other voices receded, and Sam threw Al one more despairing glance and stepped over to the bathroom door.

"*Salutari te morituris,*" he said.

Al didn't have Latin, but he spoke Italian, and he recognized the quotation and raised a fist encouragingly.

"Kiss me quick, baby!" one woman said as Sam ducked gratefully behind the barrier of the bar.

"I beg your pardon?"

Al shook his head pityingly. "It's a drink, Sam. Kiss Me Quick. Haven't you ever heard of it?"

From the look on Sam's face, it was obvious he hadn't. Al tapped ash from his cigar and started orchestrating. "You need your Pernod, and some Curaçao, and Angostura bitters, and club soda."

Sam got out the ingredients, muttering something between his teeth. Al didn't need to hear him to know what it was.

"Of course I used to tend bar. What did you expect? Okay, you mix a couple ounces, more or less, of the Pernod, a slosh of Curaçao—"

This was more than the scientist in Sam's soul could take. "How much, exactly, is a 'slosh'?"

"A little bit more than a slush and less than a lush," the customer said promptly.

"Wave the bottle over it," Al advised.

Several drops of Curaçao were added to the Pernod. Sam reached for the Angostura, hesitated.

"Just a little."

Sam added "just a little" and reached for the club soda.

"No! No, you've got to mix what you already have. That's why it's in the shaker, dummy. Add cracked ice, then put it in a brandy snifter and *then* add the club soda—there, that's right—" Al took a certain paternal pride in broadening Sam Beckett's education in these areas. Sam didn't much appreciate it, but managed a certain flourish as he presented the drink to his customer. The wave of women sloshed away.

"Could've been worse," Al observed. "She could have asked for a Bang Your Head Against the Bedpost, Baby."

Sam shot him a look of disbelief. "Are you kidding?"

"Nope." He grinned. "I never kid about things like that, Sam."

"I'd just as soon bang my head against the nearest wall, thank you," Sam muttered.

The women had retreated to a table in the middle of the room—actually several tables pushed together—and were watching the bride-to-be opening gifts. One of the advantages of being a hologram, as far as Al was concerned, was that he could always take the shortest way between two points; in this case, the point behind Sam being the first, and the woman holding the lacy black teddy up to herself being the second.

"Oooooo," Al murmured, stepping through the table. He was wickedly aware that Sam was glaring at him from across the room. "Nice pair of gabonzas."

"That'll wake him up at night," one of the women chortled.

"I'll say," Al agreed. "Tina has that one in red—"

He stopped abruptly and bit down hard on his cigar. *Tina* had that one? What about Janna?

Guilt lanced through him. He was a happily married man. Very happily married. Wasn't that the whole reason he was torn up about this Leap? So why was he acting the way he used to act?

Maybe time spent in the past with Sam didn't count?

He wasn't actually *cheating,* after all. He was just looking. He couldn't even touch—it really wasn't anything to feel guilty about, it—it wasn't fair. That blonde was *built*.

Stepping away from the cluster of women, he looked up to see Sam watching him worriedly. For some reason this only made him angry.

Sam made a show of looking for something behind the bar, then stepped out from behind it and headed for the back door.

"Wickie, baby, where you going?" one of the women called, and Sam froze like a spotlighted fawn.

"I, er, I wanted to check the kegs," he stuttered.

"Oh, let him go, Jackie, he can't get far." Rimae waved him on.

Sam waggled his eyebrows at Al, signaling him to follow. One of the women wolf-whistled. Sam fled down the narrow hallway to the door leading outside.

Al cast one more glance back at the black teddy—no, come to think of it, Tina's had a black satin ribbon right—

He yanked his attention back to the job, not without regret, and went after Sam.

He found the other man outside, draped over a stack of undersized beer kegs, his head in his hands, moaning to himself. It said a lot for the crime rate in Snow Owl, Al

189

thought, that the kegs were left outside and unprotected. "I don't want to go back in there," Sam said, not lifting his head. "I *can't* go back in there. Those women are crazy."

"Nah, they're just healthy." Al tapped impatiently on the handlink. "Ziggy, have you got anything yet?"

No. The answer was succinct.

"Well, that's certainly useful." Al looked around at the stack of kegs. "Does Rimae make a habit of leaving full kegs outside where anybody can walk off with them?"

"They're not full," Sam said wearily, straightening up. "They're empty. The full ones are back in the storeroom behind the bar, with the rest of the liquor supplies. Al, what does Ziggy say I'm supposed to *do*?"

"You talk to yourself a lot?" Rimae said. She'd followed him outside, was standing arms akimbo, looking at him.

"Yeah. A *lot*," Sam answered without missing a beat.

"Kevin Hodge's coming by soon to pick up his order, and he's getting some extra. He'll pay when he gets here. I don't want to hear any more crap like the last time, okay?" Rimae was watching him narrowly. "Just collect the money, turn over the keg and forget it, okay?"

Sam opened his mouth to protest. Al gestured frantically at the stack of empty kegs. "Just give him one of the empty ones, Sam! Fill it with water or something. Nobody'll be able to get drunk, Bethica will be okay, everything will be fine!"

Plus Bethica would have the chance to talk Kevin out of killing Wickie.

Sam caught on fast for a magnafoozled genius. "Sure, Rimae. No problem." He followed her back into the bar.

Al, in turn, followed Sam.

" . . . oh, Leezey, how wonderful! We'll be having a party for you next!"

Rimae was never one to miss an opportunity. "Which we'll have right here, of course! What are we celebrating?"

"Leezey's going to have a baby!"

"Hey, that's great!"

"I think it calls for drinks all around," the buxom brunette said. "What'll you have, Leezey?"

"I've been drinking Manhattan iced teas," Leezey said. She was still glowing from the attention. The bride-to-be was, if truth be told, glad the focus of the affair had shifted away from her for a while.

"Wickie, a Manhattan iced tea for Leezey. Girls, order up!"

"How about a nice regular iced tea instead?" Sam asked.

The silence thundered. Every woman in the place turned to stare at the bartender. Rimae's jaw dropped.

"I'm sorry," Sam said. "I didn't know you were pregnant . . . Leezey? I can't serve you any more drinks. Any more alcoholic drinks, that is."

The attention was suddenly not as welcome. Leezey turned bright red. "Why not? It's a party. I'm not driving."

"It's bad for the baby," Sam explained. He glanced quickly at Rimae. "It could create problems."

Rimae was speechless with fury.

"That's a bunch of bull," another of the women said. "I drank when I was pregnant. Everybody drinks."

"I'm sorry. I won't serve Leezey alcohol. There are a lot of other things she could drink."

"Whaddaya know, a temperance bartender," someone hooted. "Rimae, you've got a strange idea of a party here."

Sam went over to the mixers and poured a glass of ginger ale and orange juice, splashing in some cranberry juice. "You could try this," he offered.

"Only if you add some vodka," Leezey snapped. "Rimae, are you going to let him get away with this?"

Rimae marched behind the bar, took the glass away from Sam, and reached for the clear square bottle of vodka. "It's just a joke," she said. "This round is on me, girls. C'mon."

"No." Sam caught at her hand, exerting just enough force to keep her from pouring. "Don't give her that, Rimae. It'll poison the baby. Just like Davey was poisoned."

The women murmured.

Rimae jerked her hand free. "That's enough," she snapped. "You're fired, Wickie. Get the hell out of my bar."

Sam took her wrist again. "Don't do it."

Rimae's face twisted. "Either you get your hand off me, or I'm going to call the cops and have you thrown in jail. I told you to get out."

"Oh, the hell with it," Leezey said. "Mike would have my head if I came home smashed anyway. Skip the vodka, Rimae, and let's get back to the presents."

The rest of the women were more than willing to break the tension, returning to the pile of gifts with only a few looks back at Rimae and Sam. Sam finally let his hand fall away.

"You're *fired,*" Rimae snarled. "I told you to get out, and I meant it! Beat it!"

Al looked at the handlink. "Uh-oh. There goes the plan, Sam. . . ."

CHAPTER
TWENTY-ONE

"But Kevin doesn't know I've been fired," Sam insisted stubbornly to Al. He'd walked away from the party in silence, out the back door again, and they were standing near the pile of empties. "So when he comes to get the keg, all I have to do is not give it to him."

Al looked at him exasperatedly. "Sam, I don't know about you, but I never let little details like that keep me from getting booze when I wanted it."

"Then I'll talk Bethica out of going up there." He was improvising desperately now.

Al looked skeptical, but gestured with his cigar at the streetlight at the other end of the parking lot. "There she is. Be my guest."

A dozen or more young people were gathered in the yellow circle of light, with Kevin in the middle, taking up a collection. They were laughing, joking. One of the teens was Bethica. As Leaper and Observer watched, the young man wadded up several bills around a fistful of coins and started toward the Polar Bar.

"Wait until he makes the offer," Al advised. "New York isn't going to pass the twenty-one-year-old drinking age until 1990. He's not doing anything illegal. Unfortunately."

"I know," Sam said under his breath. Kevin had caught

sight of him, standing in the shadow of the eaves, and stopped a few feet away.

"Well well well," he said. "Look at that. If it isn't the Indian."

"Nice evening, Kevin," Sam said easily. "How're you doing?"

"I'm just fine," Kevin answered. The back spotlight of the bar blinked on, and even though his back was to its source Sam flinched away from the sudden glare. Kevin, caught facing it, yelped and rubbed his eyes.

"I thought so," Rimae said grimly. "Wickie, what the hell are you still doing here?"

Not waiting for an answer, she went on, "Kevin, have you got a truck to haul this thing in?"

Kevin, still blinking, grinned evilly at Wickie. "Sure do, ma'am." Turning, he waved in some of the boys. One of them got into a pickup and drove it up to the back door of the bar.

"Rimae, you can't sell to these kids," Sam said. The whole group had gathered near the door. "You know what's going to happen." They were watching, their mood still light; but Sam knew it could turn ugly in an instant, and he was wary.

"I don't sell liquor to kids," Rimae said sharply. "Kevin's nineteen. He's of age. I told you to get the hell out of here, Wickie. And I think you'd better start packing up your things, too."

Kevin chortled and counted out the money, stooping to pick up stray nickels and quarters that fell to the ground. A set of burly kids—the football team, Sam was willing to bet—followed Rimae into the bar and came out again a few minutes later with a large cask mounted on rollers. Sam reached out and grabbed Bethica by the arm, pulling her away as the boys loaded the cask into a cradle in the bed of the truck.

"Bethica, don't do it," he whispered fiercely. "Don't go. You know what happens when they get drunk."

"Yeah, and it isn't any worse than what happens when *you* get drunk," she said, pulling away. Rimae, having supervised the loading, had gone back inside.

"Hey, Bethica, you got a new boyfriend?" one of the girls mocked.

Kevin came back around the end of the truck. "What the hell? Get your hands off her."

"I'm trying to—"

"Sam. You're trying to be rational again. Rational doesn't work. I keep telling you that—"

"Leave him alone, Kevin—"

"I'm getting sick of you!"

Before Sam could figure out what was going on, he'd been pulled, pushed, shoved, and crowded to the other end of the parking lot, within the circle of light from the street lamp, and was standing in the middle of a circle of wild-eyed teenagers.

"You jerks," Al was saying bitterly. "Ziggy, give me a reading on this—oh, terrific. Sam, Ziggy says you're about to get beaten to a pulp."

"Wonderful," Sam muttered.

"The plan isn't working, Sam—"

Sam tuned him out, reaching inside himself for the calm place he needed to handle physical confrontation. He could see the faces in the circle around him, with expressions of hunger and excitement and sheer bloodlust, eyes bright, mouths slightly open, panting. Slightly behind the ring stood Bethica, the back of one hand held to her mouth, her eyes wide too, but with a different expression.

Before him, less than six feet away, Kevin, standing well balanced, smiling at him. Kevin wasn't going to let him walk away or talk his way out of a fight. He was looking forward to inflicting pain. He'd been looking forward to it for days, ever since Sam had embarrassed him in front of his friends; now he was going to erase that.

And he was going to erase Wickie too, if possible. If Bethica was supposed to go to the party to talk Kevin out

195

of trying to kill Wickie, maybe this would get it out of his system. If that was the case, maybe he could fight, lose, and Leap.

Al was still studying the handlink, talking to Ziggy, and reading out information. Sam continued to ignore him and watch Kevin, who was leaning forward slightly.

Most truly serious fights, in Sam's experience, lasted less than a minute. When someone who knew what he was doing intentionally tried to put someone else down, it didn't take long.

Kevin might or might not know what he was doing, but he wasn't trying to put Wickie down, at least not right away. He reached out and flicked Sam on the face so quickly Sam barely had time to jerk back. But then Kevin laughed and looked around for his friends' approbation, and that told Sam a great deal all by itself.

Sam contemplated finishing this mess quickly and getting back to Wickie's cabin. He hoped Rimae would change her mind; he'd hate to think he would Leap out and Wickie would return to his own body only to find himself unemployed. On the other hand, he certainly wasn't going to damage the kid, and if he didn't, Kevin would lose face, and then he'd . . .

While he was still thinking, Kevin spun around and planted a fist in his gut, propelling Sam back against the circle of spectators. They made a sound like wolves scenting blood. He barely heard it. He was too busy catching his breath.

He must give consideration to an alternative scenario, he thought dizzily as Kevin followed up with another fist to his gut. Maybe he should just let the kid win.

The second blow wasn't quite as bad as the first one, mostly because he was farther away. He struggled to get his balance back.

"Sam, are you waiting for just the right moment?" Al asked acerbically. "Because I think it was about five minutes ago."

"You're no help," Sam muttered.

Kevin looked momentarily confused, then stepped in to slug Sam in the jaw. If he could have gotten his breath back, Sam would have told him that was an extremely bad idea; fragile as the human mandible is, the human hand with all its tiny bones and network of nerve tissue is considerably more so. He didn't want Kevin to damage his hand, particularly not on Wickie's jaw. So he spun around and kicked his opponent's feet out from under him.

Both combatants went sprawling. The audience laughed.

Kevin was stunned. And furious.

By the time he was back on his feet, Sam was too. If he didn't breathe too deeply, he was okay. Balancing himself, he watched the boy warily. Bethica picked that moment to try to grab Kevin's sleeve. Kevin twisted, knocking her away. Bethica plowed right back in again.

"Kevin, stop it!"

"Sam, she's going to get hurt if this keeps up," Al said worriedly. He wasn't making a prediction based on anything Ziggy was transmitting; Sam could see for himself that Kevin wanted to hurt something, and if it wasn't going to be Wickie, it might very well be Bethica. Some of the other kids were looking at each other nervously.

He reached out and tapped Kevin on the shoulder. "Hey, kid. I'm over here. Or have you forgotten about me?"

He hadn't. He whipped around and struck Sam at the base of the throat. An inch farther up would have crushed Wickie's larynx. As it was he gagged and fell. He decided to exaggerate the consequence of the blow.

"Sam, are you okay? Sam? Sam, what happened to all those martial arts of yours? Did you Swiss-cheese the t'ai chi?"

He couldn't answer Al without spoiling his entire performance of writhing on the ground, clutching at his throat, gasping and gagging—at least he didn't have to exaggerate that part too much—and he almost missed seeing Kevin's foot draw back, heading for his ribs. Kevin's toe connected

197

hard enough to make him give a strangled yelp.

Bethica screamed. Sam rolled away, covering his head with his arms, partly to convince Kevin he was beaten and partly out of a real fear that the kid would kick him in the head next.

"Get'im, Kev!"

"Knock his lights out!"

"Stomp him!"

Apparently the kids thought so too.

The noise was enough to reach the interior of the bar. The back door opened, a rectangle of light against darkness, and the silhouette framed within it shouted, "If you kids don't get out of here I'm going to call the cops!"

It was enough to make some of the less enthusiastic start to fade away. The second warning was enough to break the spell for the rest. "C'mon, Kevin, he's beaten."

"I'm not through with him," Kevin said, low and ugly.

"Give it up, he's out of it. C'mon, she's gonna call the Man if we don't get out of here."

Sam remained tensed, all too aware of Kevin, poised to kick again. He could almost feel the boy's desire for blood, and Sam hadn't given him enough. But Bethica was murmuring urgently in his ear, and finally Kevin turned away, not without a final, "I'm not through with you, Indian!"

"Sam? Sam, are you okay?"

Al had been talking for some time, Sam realized, helpless in the knowledge that he couldn't touch his friend, couldn't communicate with him. Sam peeked out from under his arm to see feet receding, except of course for Al's silver running shoes. After a moment he could hear vehicle doors slamming, engines revving; he hid his face again just in time to protect his eyes from a spray of gravel.

Moments later the rear parking lot was empty except for Leaper and hologram. Sam rolled over on his back, ignoring the small rocks that dug into him, and stretched out his arms.

"Sam!" Al was beginning to sound as hoarse as Sam felt.

Sam waved a placating hand at him. "I'm okay," he croaked. "I'm fine, Al. Really." He sighed and rolled up to his feet in one less-than-smooth movement. "Except I guess I've totally blown it."

Al stood staring at him. "You're crazy. Has anybody ever told you you're crazy?"

"Besides you?" Sam felt at his throat, rubbed his ribs. Nothing broken, no thanks to Kevin. "I'm getting kind of old for this, aren't I?" A thought struck him. "How old am I, anyway?"

"You *are* crazy," Al muttered. "That kid just beat you half to death and you want to know how old you are?"

Sam coughed experimentally. No blood. Another good sign. "Oh, come on. He didn't even come close." A stab of pain reminded him that he hadn't exactly gotten off without a scratch, either. "I'm serious. How old *am* I, Al? When is it now?"

Al opened his mouth to give the answer, looked down at his link with Ziggy, and reconsidered. "Well, I could tell you the date, but I don't know if that will tell you how much time you've actually experienced. Do you age in between Leaps?"

Glaring, Sam shook his head. "It was 1995 when I Leaped. When is it now?"

Al shrugged. "2005."

"So I'm going to be . . ." Sam calculated the difference between the year 2005 and the year of his birth, 1953, and decided he didn't really want to think about the answer after all. "No wonder I'm slowing up a little."

CHAPTER
TWENTY-TWO

"Not too much, I hope," Al said grimly, studying the handlink. "She's going up with them to the same place in the mountains they were last Friday."

Was it only last Friday? Sam thought, dazed. He took a step toward Wickie's cabin and the Polar Bar truck, and staggered. "Oh, boy," he muttered.

"He hurt you worse than you thought," Al observed.

"No kidding." Sam drew in a deep breath, winced, and started moving.

" 'Into the Valley of Death' . . ."

"Just bring the shield, Sancho, okay?"

"He *must* have hit you harder than I thought," Al said. "You don't usually mix your cues that way."

"It can't be any worse than those drinks," he shot back, and paused to catch his breath while catching hold of the driver's side door. He had some vague idea of following Bethica and keeping her from getting hurt, but had no idea how.

Something would turn up. Something always did. He got into the truck, started it up, and pulled out, rattling over the ruts, his breath catching at the jabs of pain. Al hovered indecisively, then summoned the Door. "I'd better go back and see if Ziggy's got anything better than this," he said.

Sam glanced over at him. "I hope—"

He paused, awkwardly. He wasn't sure what he hoped.

He wasn't sure he really remembered Janna. There was a hole in his memory for that party that wouldn't happen for another eighteen years. She mattered to his best friend, and that ought to be enough, but if he succeeded tonight, he'd be taking her away from him just as surely as if—

"Say hello for me," he said lamely.

"I will if she's there," Al said evenly. He moved into the Door and glanced back at Sam, took a deep breath, and added, "Good luck."

The whirling of time stopped, the lights on the handlink faded out, and Al stood alone in the Imaging Chamber, listening to the humming of the air circulator and the power that kept the Project going.

Clearing his throat, he said tentatively, "Ziggy?"

"I'm here, Admiral." As if the computer would be anywhere else.

"What's the situation, Ziggy?" His voice was stronger now. He was used to asking for situation reports, after all. He'd done it for years, and sometimes the situation was more desperate than this.

"There is no change insofar as your relationship with Mrs. Calavicci goes. However . . . you may wish to meet with Dr. Beeks to review the additional data I've developed."

When would it be *over*, he thought. When would "goodbye" finally be "goodbye"?

"O . . . kay." He squared his shoulders and left the Imaging Chamber.

"No change. My projection is that because of her discussion with Kevin about the fight with Wickie, she'll be sufficiently distraught that she'll lose control of her vehicle and crash, resulting in a non-fatal accident which severs her spine.

She'll also," the computer added as an afterthought, "lose her child in the process."

"She's pregnant?" Al was startled out of his grim focus.

Verbeena winced. "Oh, that poor baby!" It wasn't clear to any of them whether she was referring to Bethica or to her baby. She got up and poured herself a cup of coffee from her office dispenser.

"At the moment," Ziggy advised.

Al opened his mouth, closed it again. He tried again. "Ziggy, did you happen to trace that kid when you were trying to figure out the connection with—"

Ziggy was fast. "I have now, Admiral. Bethica's child is, indeed, the connection."

"She is?" Verbeena said. "Then we've got it figured out! That's great!"

Al schooled himself into impassivity. "How?"

"If the child is born, she'll grow up and apply to college. She has an excellent relationship with her guidance counselor, one Janna Fulkes, and asks Ms. Fulkes to accompany her on her orientation visit to Yale. Ms. Fulkes agrees, even though it delays her reporting to her new job in the personnel department of Project Quantum Leap until June twentieth, 1993. By which time you will already be involved with Tina Martinez-O'Farrell."

Verbeena glanced at him and looked discreetly away.

Despite himself, Al sighed, a small weary tobacco-tinged breath escaping between his lips. "It's my own fault, isn't it?"

"It was a choice you made." Ziggy's tone was neither accusing nor approving. Its very neutrality was almost more than Al could take.

"So she's still there, but as soon as I go tell Sam and he figures out how to fix things for the kid—"

"There's a ninety-eight-percent chance that this present will disappear."

"Why did it appear to begin with?" Al demanded. "Why did I have this, at least for a while?"

"When Dr. Beckett Leaped in, there was no resonance at all. As soon as he arrived, the ripple effect started as a result of minor changes, which in turn gave rise to the child never being born, or never applying to Yale, or any of a dozen other possibilities. In each case the future proceeded as you can see."

Al considered. He wasn't in the same class as Sam Beckett, but he was very far from stupid. "That's a logical impossibility, Ziggy. You're saying that originally, there was no accident, the kid lived, Janna was late, I got together with Tina and never married Janna. But Sam arrived, so as a result Bethica gets into an argument that incidentally causes the kid to die, so Janna's on time to get her job, I meet her, and we get married?"

"Are you telling me that child is *supposed* to die?" Verbeena snapped.

"I doubt that," Ziggy said, dissatisfied. "As soon as he arrived, things changed." The computer paused. "I can only assume that in the greater order of things, this child was supposed to live. And God or Fate or Chance or Time or whatever causes Dr. Beckett to Leap is just getting around to putting this particular second-order error right."

"But wait a minute," Al protested, "if that was the case, I should have been married to Janna all along, and my getting involved with *Tina* should be the ripple effect." He got up and crossed over to the markerboard. The stink of the marker filled Verbeena's office as he twisted off the top and began to try to illustrate it with blue Venn diagrams.

Verbeena looked understandably confused, so he tried again. "Look. No Sam"—a circle with a smiley face and a slash through it—"equals no fight"—a mass of squeaking Xs—"equals baby okay"—a smaller smiley face, unmarred—"equals Janna late"—a frowning face—"and I'm with Tina." Tina was represented by a squiggly hourglass. "Everything's copacetic." He paused to look at the board, couldn't figure out how to illustrate copacetic, and continued.

"Sam Leaps in, his just being there—Sam being Sam—guarantees a fight, Bethica's in an accident, there's no baby. The future changes. I'm married to Janna." The board was covered with arrows, circles, slashes, Xs. He took a moment to make sure he had everything right. "Sam *couldn't* have Leaped in to make sure Bethica didn't get hurt in the accident; she never *had* an accident until he showed up. Whatever he has to put right, that isn't it."

"But now he has to fix that too," Verbeena said, thinking the board looked like a particularly messy football play diagram.

Unwillingly, Al nodded.

"Then we still don't know what Sam's supposed to put right," Verbeena said thoughtfully. "Ziggy?"

"I have no idea," the computer admitted.

"Well, you'd better figure it out pretty soon," Verbeena pointed out. "Didn't you say he was going up there when you left them? And wasn't Kevin going to try to kill Wickie?"

"That's correct, Dr. Beeks."

Verbeena looked inquiringly at Al. "You got a reason to stick around here, honey?"

He got to his feet. "Just one, as it happens."

He wanted a cigar in the worst way, but he couldn't smoke here. And it would have made such a great distraction, too.

"She's waiting for you," Ziggy said.

There had to be a feminine side to either Beckett or Calavicci, Verbeena thought, to give Ziggy that exquisite sensitivity. She watched Al go, wondering how on earth he could stand to do what he had to do.

There was, however, one more issue she'd like to have resolved. "Ziggy," she said quietly. "Who's the father of Bethica's child? Is it Kevin?"

Ziggy paused. "There's a ninety-nine-percent chance that the father is . . . Wickie Starczynski."

• • •

She was waiting for him at the bottom of the ramp, as if she knew there was something different about this time, something important. He came up to her and took her hands and kissed her lightly on the tip of the nose. "Hey, sweetheart."

Her blue eyes were troubled. "Hey, sweetheart."

He didn't know what to say. He had a hundred things he could say, and none of them, not one, seemed appropriate. He had a sudden image of the airport scene in *Casablanca,* a flash of memory of Seymour, the kid who wanted excitement and got more than he'd bargained for, whose view of life was shaped by Mickey Spillane and dime novels. Any second now he was going to hear himself saying something like, "the troubles of two people don't amount to a hill of beans in this world."

She knew something was wrong, badly wrong, and she wanted him to share it with her, knew he wouldn't.

The only mercy in all of this, he thought, was that Janna, like Verbeena, wouldn't remember once the past was changed back. They weren't linked to Ziggy, whom God or Fate or Chance or Whatever had thrown outside of Time so Sam could Leap, making things right.

And sometimes making things wrong that accidentally went right in the process.

He would be left with the memories of such a short time—a shopping trip to Santa Fe, liquid honey, comfort after bad dreams, quarters that looked more like a home than an institution.

Tina was a delight. Had been. Would be. She was in his future, the future he'd been used to, had enjoyed before and would again. But it wouldn't be Janna.

But if he didn't do this, he'd regret it. Maybe not today, maybe not tomorrow . . .

"I love you very much, you know that?" he said softly.

"Of course I do," she said. "Al?"

"Have I ever shown you the Imaging Chamber?" he asked.

"What exactly is your relationship with Bethica Hoffman, Mr. Starczynski?" Verbeena Beeks in the throes of an attack of motherliness was not to be denied. She'd never met Bethica Hoffman; she didn't have to. She'd swept in—literally; her caftan caught on a chair and she kicked it aside without a second thought—and marched over to the diagnostic bed upon which the Visitor was lying. Now she was standing, arms akimbo, staring down at him.

The man in the Waiting Room shot her a wary glance, setting aside the magazine he was reading—an old issue of a popular science magazine. "Who wants to know?"

"I do." Verbeena Beeks was not in the mood to take any back talk from a Visitor. "This young lady is a minor child, and she's pregnant, and I have reason to believe you're the father."

"Holy sh—How do you know?" The face that was Sam Beckett's was white with shock. It was enough to convince Verbeena that Ziggy was right. Wickie Starczynski sat upright. He would have gotten to his feet, but Verbeena didn't allow him the room. Her snapping brown glare pinned him to the bed.

"That doesn't matter," she said evenly. "What *does* matter is just what you plan to do about it."

"Hey, it wasn't my fault—"

"Oh, really," Verbeena said dryly. "Last I heard, it takes two." Now that she'd gotten his attention, she stepped away, striding to the opposite side of the room.

"She came on to me! She broke up with that fancy boyfriend of hers because she finally found out what he was really like, and she came to me to make sure he'd leave Davey alone, and—I guess she was mad. She thought she'd show him. She was crying. And, and it just kind of . . . happened. I'm not saying it was right." He was on his feet immediately, but he knew better than to follow her.

"Do you even care about her?" Verbeena was making an elaborate show of glancing through a stack of other books and magazines on the table. An interesting, if eclectic, collection: *Psychology Today, New Discoveries,* the math books they'd been working with, *Call of the Wild.* Crossword puzzles. She looked up just in time to see the look on his face.

"Of course I care about her," he was saying bitterly. "But what difference does that make? I'm just a half-breed bartender."

It was the wrong thing to say, and definitely the wrong person to say it to.

"Pretty soon"—*I hope*, she added prayerfully to herself—"you're going to be going back to yourself. I think you better start thinking about how you're going to handle the situation you're going to be walking into. Just what do you plan to do about it?"

"What do you mean?"

He only had an eighth-grade education, Verbeena reminded herself.

But he also had a mind. And if he had a mind, he could do anything.

And he was going to get a determined push toward using it, right here, right now.

"This is where you stand?" Janna said, pirouetting around on the disk. "What do you see?"

"I see Sam. I see wherever he is—" He thought with a pang about the bachelorette party in the Polar Bar.

Janna caught the gleam in his eye. "And just where is that?" she said with mock sternness.

Al shrugged. "Wherever he is." Halfway up the mountain by now, he thought. In fact he'd probably already arrived at Kevin's little party in progress. He had to get going.

"Could I see, too?" she asked, predictably.

"I'm afraid not," he said. "I can only see him because of a subatomic agitation of carbon quarks tuned to the mesons of Sam's optic and otic neurons. . . ."

Janna burst out laughing. "Your *what*? *Carbon* quarks? Oh, come on, even I know better than that."

Al shrugged. "What can I say, it worked on Congress." He found himself pulling out a cigar, unwrapping it. "Janna, love, I have to go now—"

Caught in the midst of examining the translucent white panels that made up the Chamber's walls, she turned back to him. "Go? Go where?"

He shook his head. "I mean, you have to go. Out. I have to get back to Sam."

Puzzled, she knit her brows. "Okay, Al. I'm glad you showed me this. I've always wondered what it looked like."

"It looks exactly like this." He gestured widely with the hand holding the cigar. The handlink was beginning to light up. "Janna, it's time."

"All right." She stepped over to the air-lock door through the Accelerator, looked back at him. "Al? Will you be back in time for dinner?"

He bit his lip. "I don't think so. Go ahead without me, okay?"

"Okay." She ran to him suddenly and gave him a quick fierce hug. "Love you."

He returned the embrace, kissing the top of her head. "Love you back, honey."

She ran back to the air-lock door, gave him a quick wave. "See you soon!"

He raised his hand as if to say farewell, and punched the handlink control instead. "Center me on Sam, Ziggy," he said roughly. "Now."

CHAPTER
TWENTY-THREE

There just wasn't any way to park the truck closer. He left it at about the same place it had been on Friday night. He wondered where the kids were parking.

He passed the pine branch, which slapped him in the face again.

He was ready for the clearing, and he paused to scope out the situation before charging in.

Two campfires, as before; almost two dozen people scattered around. Somehow Kevin had brought a truck around, too—he could see the road now, on the other side of the clearing. Kevin himself sat on the tailgate, swinging his legs and holding forth on something or other to a group of six or seven teens.

By one fire a young woman played plaintive sixties folk songs on an acoustic guitar. Her audience, another girl and a boy, was more interested in each other than in the music. Not far away a cluster of boys were chugging from cans. Someone was toasting marshmallows over the other fire— he caught the smell of burning sugar and swallowed against a rush of saliva, remembering too late he'd skipped dinner. Someone else had a radio, tuned to the harder rock of the current decade.

He couldn't seem to find Bethica. He looked them over

again. They were quiet still, the clashing music the loudest part of it. She wasn't there.

No, there she was, coming down that road. Sam started to step out from the trees, then stopped, waiting to see what would happen first.

They were expecting her. If he strained, he could hear the greetings. It helped that the radio got staticky and someone turned it off just about the time the greetings were over.

"So Bethie baby, gonna have one?" Kevin said, holding a paper cup under a spigot.

She held out a hand, took the cup. Sam made himself stay still. This wasn't what he was supposed to change. Not this.

Besides, she looked at it and set it down on the fender of the truck. "No thanks."

Sam, watching, felt a rush of relief, and even some pride. She *had* listened after all.

"Oh, c'mon. What's the matter, you want something harder?" Kevin produced a bottle.

Someone else laughed and staggered. The bottle was half-empty.

"No thanks."

"So what the hell you want?" Kevin said. "You swear off or something?"

"Maybe later," she responded, looking around, away.

"Later might be too late," Kevin said, nudging one of his friends. "I have some unfinished business to take care of." They laughed immoderately.

"What unfinished business?"

Sam leaned forward. He thought he knew the answer already, but it never hurt to be sure. He was still moving stiffly. If Kevin was going to go after him again, he was going to have to stop holding back and really use the body he was occupying.

Poor Wickie. He wondered if the guy was really used to all this exercise.

"I'm going to take care of that Indian." Kevin tilted his head back and drank directly from the bottle. Sam could

212

see the amber liquid glinting in the light from the fires as the level dropped.

"I'm gonna take care of him good," Kevin went on, wiping the whiskey from his mouth. "You think tonight was a fight? That was just a taste. I'm gonna pound him so hard—"

Sam's eyes narrowed. It was unlikely that Wickie would allow this kid to "pound" him. Sam had no intention of allowing it, either, but he was less concerned about it at the moment than in keeping an eye on Bethica.

His own rules for Quantum Leaping were designed to minimize the effect of observation on the events observed. It wasn't necessary to intervene here in order to keep Bethica from getting in an automobile accident; the best approach he could think of at the moment was just to keep an eye on her, and when she left, talk her into going with him rather than driving herself. All he had to do was get her home safely tonight, and then he could Leap.

"No, you won't," Bethica said suddenly. "You're just a drunken bully, you know that, Kevin Hodge? You think you're such a big deal because you can buy booze. Because you can *hit* people." Her face was twisted with loathing.

The kids gathered around Kevin fell silent, looking at each other and at their leader, waiting to see what he would do. Kevin set down his bottle and slipped down from the tailgate. Sam tensed. Getting Bethica home safely didn't include letting Kevin hurt her.

"What's the matter, your big crush isn't a big enough man to protect himself?" he jeered. "He's just another gutless Indian. I'm sure your friend Wickie would like to take my scalp, but he can't sneak up behind me to get it!"

He looked around, encouraging his sycophants' laughter. They laughed, obediently, but didn't look very happy about it. Sam waited.

"Yeah, you used to pretend you were part Indian when you were in the second grade," Bethica pointed out. "Remember? You did a lot of sneaking then. Now all you can do is beat people up. And he's never done anything to you."

"Like hell he didn't," Kevin said with sudden fury. "He tried to make a fool of me. I don't take that from anybody, especially not some damn bartender."

"I don't think it's last Friday that's bothering you at all, is it? It's Wickie. Last Friday was just—"

One of the girls in the group laughed. "Bethie has a crush on Wickie!"

"I do not!"

It was amazing, Sam thought, how quickly a teenager—or a group of teenagers—could regress to acting like six-year-olds. They crowded around Bethica making verbal jabs about her supposed relationship with Wickie, and she denied them all, getting more and more red in the face and finally crying. If he walked out in that clearing now, he realized, he'd probably completely ruin her reputation for good. He had to let her battle it out by herself, and as long as she wasn't suffering any physical harm, he would.

He started moving back, to go around the clearing and find out where she'd parked, to keep her from getting in her car and driving off. In the state of mind she was in at the moment, he could well imagine she wouldn't be paying too much attention to her driving.

He could still hear the laughter from the clearing as he worked his way around; it didn't yet have the particular ugly undertone of violence. Bethica was still protesting, from the sound of it, perhaps too much.

"Bethie's got it bad for Wickie!"

"How is he, Bethica?"

"What's Rimae gonna say? I hear she kinda likes him too."

"She's gonna run away to the reservation with Wickie!"

"She's gonna raise papooses!"

That one was the straw that broke the camel's back. Bethica pushed her way out of her circle of tormentors and began running up the dirt road. She went past just as Sam fought his way out from the brush.

"Bethica?" he called, trying to pitch his voice to reach

the weeping girl without attracting the attention of the occupants of the clearing. He didn't think much of anything would get their attention now, though; they were celebrating Bethica's rout, not pursuing her.

"Bethica!" Unfortunately, Bethica didn't know that; what she must have seen with her blurred vision was something dark, terrifying, looming at her from the direction of the clearing. She screamed and bolted.

Sam found himself chasing her down the dirt road, past the vehicles parked at random angles. Wickie was in good shape; Sam had had occasion to test that over the past three days; but Bethica was frightened, running like a gazelle, and Sam had to push himself to catch her.

"Beth-i-ca—it's me, Wickie!"

Bethica wasn't listening. They were past the turnoff to the paved road now, and the "road" had dwindled to no more than a rapidly narrowing path. He tried to catch at the fringes of her vest.

She gasped and veered away, toward the tall brush and trees at the side of the road.

And vanished.

Sam tried to skid to a halt. As a result, he was completely off balance when he toppled through the hole in the brush Bethica had made.

He expected to hit the ground hard, and tried to relax into the fall. This would have worked, had there been any ground to hit.

Instead he toppled down a small cliff and landed on top of Bethica, who screamed again and beat at him.

"Hey, wait a minute!" He managed to catch hold of her flailing fists in the dark. "Bethica, calm down! It's Wickie! Come on, Bethica!"

Her frantic efforts to defend herself against the monster from the dark froze. Sam managed to get himself untangled from her, then froze himself as rocks slipped and his right foot pawed for purchase on thin air. "Ohboy."

Bethica deflated back into tears.

Sam cautiously brought himself back onto solid ground. "Are you okay?" he asked, wedging the two of them closer to the slope they'd fallen down. He could barely see the glimmer of moonlight reflected off the skin of her face, and it was marred by shadows.

He twisted around to sit beside her and brushed at those shadows, relieved to find only dirt and the dampness of tears instead of blood. "Are you okay?" he asked again.

"I'm fine. Ow."

"There's an inherent contradiction in that," Al observed.

Sam jumped, not least because Al looked like a ghost, standing in the light of the Imaging Chamber. That light didn't illuminate the ledge Sam and Bethica were sitting on; Al stood in a shimmer all his own. If it weren't for the cigar stuck in the middle of his mouth, he might have been mistaken for a heavenly apparition.

Sam knew better. He grimaced, unable to respond to the hologrammic image, and went back to Bethica. "Where does it hurt?" he asked, shifting around carefully. He was sitting on rocks and branches, and it was damned uncomfortable. "Is everything okay?" The question didn't make much sense for Bethica, but it wasn't intended for the girl anyway.

Al surveyed the man and girl before him and shook his head. "Not exactly."

At the same time, Bethica sniffled, "My ankle—"

Sam leaned forward cautiously. "Which one?"

As he unwound Bethica's leg out from under her and probed gingerly at her ankle, Al provided a summary of the situation. "—So we're kind of back where we started, Sam," he finished, just as Bethica yelped in affirmation.

"That's it?" Sam asked his patient. "Or is there more?"

She wiped at her nose, nearly elbowing him in the eye in the process.

Al assumed the question was for him. "Ziggy thinks you still have to keep Bethica from getting hurt, but that's a second-order change."

"Is that all?" he said patiently.

"Uh-huh." Al's voice and Bethica's blended in an eerie chorus.

"Can you wiggle your toes?"

Sniff. "Yes."

"I think it's just a sprain," he diagnosed. "I could tell better if I could *see* anything."

"Well, can't you—" Bethica began, trying to get up on her good foot.

Sam caught her just before she toppled down into the unknown depths. "Hold on!"

She held on. He pulled her back onto the ledge and began feeling around them, shooting Al an aggrieved look.

"Don't go glaring at *me*, Sam, *I* don't know where the heck you are," the Observer snapped. "Nobody recorded the precise location of this particular piece of real estate. There are some real bad dropoffs along that path. I think you'd better stay put until you can see better."

"Oh, great." Sam settled his shoulders against the back of their oasis and pulled Bethica into his arms to make sure she didn't try any more lunges. "Bethica, I think it's just a sprain, okay? But neither one of us can see well enough to figure out how to get out of where we are, and even if your friends were disposed to help us"—

Al snorted.

—"I don't think they could hear us if we yelled. I'm sorry, but I think we're going to have to spend the night here."

"They'd probably push you over the cliff," Al muttered acerbically.

Bethica curled up against him, her head fitting under his chin. Under Wickie's chin, he reminded himself. Bethica was acting very . . . comfortable.

"That's pretty cozy, Sam," Al remarked. "Looks like she's had some practice."

Sam glared, and stilled his hand, which was resting all too familiarly on Bethica's tangled hair. "You've got leaves and stuff here," he muttered. "Hold still and let me get them out. It's going to be okay. I promise you."

"Mostly," Al murmured around his cigar. "Almost everybody gets happily ever after in this one."

"Does that mean you're going to marry me, or something?" she demanded. "I thought you said that was a dumb idea."

"*I'm* going to marry—" Sam exchanged a panicked look with the Observer.

"It's your baby," Al said, looking at the handlink. "Wickie's, I mean. Thanks a *lot,* Ziggy, we could have used that a little earlier."

A light dawned for Sam Beckett, and he looked over Bethica's head at the hologram. "Kevin knows you were with Wi—with me, doesn't he? That's why he hates me so much."

She half nodded. "I guess it was pretty dumb. Telling him." She paused. "I am just a kid still, I guess."

Sam hugged her. "Did he know about the baby then?"

"No. I told him today. It made him even more mad. He almost wants the baby to be his. But he's afraid it's yours."

Sam sighed. A lot of things were clearer now. But it wasn't going to make the next eight hours any easier.

TUESDAY

June 10, 1975

. . . never send to know for whom the bell tolls; it tolls for thee.

—John Donne, Devotions XVII

CHAPTER

TWENTY-FOUR

Flustered or not, Sam had to act as if he knew all about Bethica and Wickie's past physical relationship, brief though it had been. Al and Ziggy were unable to help; there weren't any records, no father recorded for a baby who had, in the original history, never been born. All they had was Verbeena's discussion with the Visitor. He'd had a lot of practice pretending, though, and Bethica couldn't see the sometimes panicked expression on his face either.

He finally got her calmed down. After a while they both fell asleep. Al looked down on them, hand poised above the handlink to open the Door and return to the Imaging Chamber; after a moment he sighed, tugged his fedora over his eyes, and sat down on empty air, prepared to take the night watch.

"Who told you you couldn't go back to school?" Verbeena said impatiently. She had no intention of letting up on the Project's involuntary guest. "Which part of it is impossible? Walking up to the door? Signing the form? Sitting in a desk? *Listening* to somebody?

"Or are you just one of those men who runs out on pregnant women?"

"It's not my fault," Wickie repeated. He didn't like it. He

made it clear he didn't like it. He tried to withdraw in stony silence.

Verbeena wouldn't have it. "What, you're scared? Child, you have no *idea* about scared. Scared is being a little girl with a baby and no idea in the world what she's gonna do about it. You're smart. Look at all you've done! Are you gonna bury yourself behind a bar, drink yourself to death, and prove all those nasty words they say are true?"

Wickie glared. "I don't even know for sure that it's mine!"

"But you broke off with Rimae as soon as it happened, didn't you?" she said shrewdly.

Wickie sputtered.

Verbeena kept hammering, hoping to spark smoldering resentment into flame.

They woke, stiff and sore, in the light of morning, to find that only a few feet farther along, the cliff down which they'd fallen softened into a slope gentle enough to climb. Sam helped the girl up and then looked over their night's refuge.

"I guess it wasn't so bad after all," he said with false heartiness.

"That's because you haven't looked over on this side," Al remarked. Sam looked up, startled. "I decided to see this one through," the hologram muttered, stretching and scratching at the grizzled stubble on his chin. He pointed to the side opposite the one they'd climbed. A few inches to the other side of the ledge they'd spent the night on, a ravine at least sixty feet deep yawned.

Sam decided to be grateful for small favors, and draping Bethica's arm around his neck, they started back for the clearing.

Not surprisingly, most of the cars parked along the dirt road were gone, including the one in which Bethica had come. "I guess one of the others took it back." Two of the partyers were still stretched out by the blackened embers of the campfires. Neither one was Kevin.

One of the boys looked at them blearily. "Hey, lookit. It's Bethie. You okay, Bethie?"

They seemed to have forgotten the gauntlet of the night before, or at least weren't willing to resume their teasing in front of Wickie. That was fine with Sam, and with Bethica as well.

"Where's Kevin?" the other boy asked. "Ooooh, my head hurts!"

"He probably went home if he had any sense," Al said.

"He went looking for you after a while, but he didn't find you. I think he decided to leave when the booze ran out," the first boy said. "He was going up the mountain to his parents' cabin up by the run. I forget when."

"Fine," Sam muttered. He and Bethica both wanted to get home; Bethica was making noises about bathrooms, and Sam empathized. The two of them staggered on to the Polar Bar truck and got in.

It was a lot easier to find his way back to the road in the light of early morning. He managed to miss most of the potholes on the way back to the pavement. The roof of the cab was never going to be the same, though.

"Could you, um, kind of hurry?" Bethica asked, not looking at him.

"Could you kind of wrap this up?" Al said, sticking his head through the rear window to appear between them. "I'd suggest you get a move on. There's somebody behind you, and I don't think he's friendly."

They had just passed the place where, the previous Friday, Sam had gone all over the road in an effort not to hit the squirrel. He glanced in the rearview to confirm Al's information; as he suspected, it was Kevin, in a fire engine red Ford truck.

"He must have been waiting for us," Sam muttered.

"Who?" Bethica asked.

"See if you can get your seat belt on," he said. "I wonder how he knew?"

Al tapped at the handlink. "Who knows? Maybe he went looking for you guys and saw you over the edge. I didn't see him, though. Still, he must know this mountain like the back of his hand. He'd figure you'd climb out in the morning." He studied the handlink. "I hope you're a really good driver, Sam. Ziggy says it's ninety-nine percent now that *this* is the accident Bethica gets hurt in."

If Sam could have spared the attention, he might have asked what happened to Wickie. Al wasn't mentioning Wickie. Sam decided he really didn't want to know, and concentrated on his driving.

Kevin was pushing, just a little, tailgating them, nudging the truck's back bumper. His vehicle was a heavy truck, massing less than the Polar Bar's but more than enough to push them off the road. His driving was erratic, wobbling. He was drunk.

Sam hugged the side of the mountain, refusing to let Kevin push him into going too fast for the mountain road. He could remember too well the sickening feeling of lost control. "I hope he didn't mess with the brakes," he asked Al as directly as possible. He was wishing, too, that he'd replaced the seat belt as well as the burned-out headlight.

Al punched in the query. "Ziggy says no. Ziggy also says Verbeena's working on Wickie. She thinks that has something to do with what has to be fixed."

A flash of disjointed memory of arguments lost from long ago came to Sam. "Poor Wickie," he muttered.

"What do you mean?" Bethica was still struggling with the seat belt, in between turning around to try to see behind them.

"Never mind," he answered, his tone grim. Kevin was trying to get between them and the cliff, and on the last hairpin turn he had nearly succeeded. They were heading toward the last switchback before going into town now, and the dropoff was going to be on their side of the road.

"Ziggy says there's a good chance you're all going to buy the farm on this one," Al advised.

"That's so comforting," Sam said between his teeth. He had one more idea, but it depended on flaws, just as everything else in this Leap had been flawed. He slowed down again, and Bethica yipped as the red truck jolted them.

"Do you have your seat belt fastened?" he asked her.

"Y-yes," she said. Her fingers were digging into the cushion of the bench seat. "Wickie, you don't have to marry me, or anything, if we get out of this."

The handlink squealed. "Oh, that's interesting. Verbeena has just told Wickie about high school equival"—Al whacked the handlink—"lency tests, and—" He fell silent.

Sam risked a glance at him. "Al?"

Al shook his head, stuck his cigar in his mouth at a jaunty angle and said, "Well, that's the easiest divorce I've ever had."

"I'm sorry," Sam whispered.

"Easy come, easy go," the Observer responded. "You still have to keep yourself from getting killed, Sam. Where's your seat belt?"

"It got broken," he said between his teeth. The truck jolted again, and Sam nearly lost it. He focused on his driving, wishing he picked Formula II driving as a hobby instead of karate—what did anybody need with more than one martial art anyway? In any event, he didn't need to look at his friend to know the look in Al's eyes.

The rising sun cast sharp shadows across the road, and they came up on the boulder in the road into the full glare of its rays. This was the place, Sam knew; this was it, win or lose, do or—No. They weren't going to lose. He slowed down to take the turn wide, staying away from the dropoff to his right. He could hear the roar of the engine behind him, coming up one last time for the final push over the cliff.

Sam stomped on the brakes.

The Polar Bar truck screeched to the left, and Sam steered frantically, not into the skid this time but away from it, encouraging the heavy truck to swing around. The vehicle behind them suddenly had nothing to hit—and not enough room to stop.

The Polar Bar truck slammed sideways into the solid rock face of the cliff, facing back up the way they'd come, jolting Sam nearly through the door.

The red truck sailed through the crash barrier and over the cliff.

Sam and Bethica watched it go, silent, listening to it hit. Sam closed his eyes against the memory of the brown-haired kid, alive and vibrant and, and *alive,* dammit, and he reached out for Bethica's hand to remind himself that he hadn't just set Kevin up only to save himself. It wasn't like Maggie and Tom. It wasn't. Bethica unsnapped the seat belt and grabbed his arm, peering through the window at the column of smoke rising from the gorge below.

"Oh, no," she whispered. "Kevin . . ."

"That's it," Al announced, examining the handlink. "Bethica and her baby survive"—he slanted a glance to the girl—"even if she doesn't believe it yet. You can Leap, Sam."

Sam took a deep breath and tried to quit shuddering. "What about—"

"Ziggy says there were two things that needed to be fixed on this Leap. The second one was yours—saving Bethica and the baby. So she'll grow up and call on her favorite counselor for help during orientation." There was no particular emotion in Al's voice as he said it.

"But . . ." Sam was ignoring Bethica's wide eyes. He took her into his arms and tucked her head under his chin.

"The first thing was getting the baby's father to marry Bethica. No, I guess that really would have been second, wouldn't it. Ziggy says to do that Wickie had to be convinced he could do something with his life. And that was a job for *Verbeena.* It took both of you this time. You had to Leap in to send Wickie back to Verbeena, and at the same time save Bethica and the baby. Wickie and Bethica do okay. They have three more kids, in fact."

"But—"

"I know. I know. So why haven't you Leaped? I don't know."

"I think I do," Sam muttered. His lips brushed Bethica's hair, and she sat up slowly to look at him. "Bethica? It's over. You're okay. The baby's going to be okay too. It's all right."

She still didn't cry well. "How do you know?" she demanded, through a veil of matted hair and tears.

Sam took a deep breath. "Because I'm going to marry you." He smiled, thinking of Rimae as Wickie's mother-in-law. She was a tough woman, but a good one. It might be a shock, but he thought she'd get used to it.

Bethica was shocked out of her tears, anyway. "Really?"

"Really," he said. "I promise. And if I forget I promised"—he rubbed his head and gave an entirely sincere wince—"you have to remind me. All right?"

"If I do you have to go to school," she said, ever practical.

"I'll go to school, too."

"Promise?"

"I can't imagine you're going to let me forget."

She smiled, shaky but brave, and reached out one hand to touch his face. "You're a good man, Wickie Gray Wolf."

"Nothing like the love of a good woman," Al said sadly, and waved goodbye as Sam Leaped.